JUNGLE DOGS

YEARLING BOOKS are designed especially to entertain and enlighten young people. Patricia Reilly Giff, consultant to this series, received her bachelor's degree from Marymount College and a master's degree in history from St. John's University. She holds a Professional Diploma in Reading and a Doctorate of Humane Letters from Hofstra University. She was a teacher and reading consultant for many years, and is the author of numerous books for young readers.

JUNGLE DOGS

Graham
Salisbury

A YEARLING BOOK

Published by
Bantam Doubleday Dell Books for Young Readers
a division of
Random House, Inc.
1540 Broadway
New York, New York 10036

Visit us on the Web! www.randomhouse.com

Educators and librarians, for a variety of teaching tools, visit us at www.randomhouse.com/teachers

ISBN: 0-440-41573-X

Reprinted by arrangement with Delacorte Press

Printed in the United States of America

December 1999

10 9 8 7 6 5 4 3

OPM

For Robyn,
who loves dogs,
and whose support and patience
are a gift I cherish

1

FAR OUT ON THE OCEAN a small reef of clouds sat still and silent over a black sea, just above where the sun would rise. A crimson fire was burning along its lower edge. The rest of the night sky was a receding deep purple black, now almost empty of stars. Under these dark heavens Boy Kahekilimaikalani Regis and his older brother, Damon, sat on their bikes, looking down a narrow dirt road that curved into a stretch of jungle.

Boy leaned forward and squinted into the shadowy trees and thick twisty weeds. He could feel his heart thumping high in his throat. "What . . . what if they're in there?" he said.

"What if who's in there?"

"Jungle dogs. What if they're in there?"

Damon kicked his foot out. "Pow! Kick 'um. Like that."

It was still too dark for Boy to see much, but even if he could he wasn't about to go in there.

1

Not now, not tomorrow, not ever. What made it worse was that no matter how he felt about it, he had to do it. It was *his* job, now. His. Not Damon's.

"I can't," Boy said.

"Just kick 'um, I tell you. Send 'um yelping." Damon's voice was deep and whispery smooth. "Come on, man. You can do it." He grinned at Boy and flicked his eyebrows.

Damon wasn't scared of anything. He was the leader of his own gang of Kailua street boys, the Cudas. Boy wasn't one of them.

Boy looked down at his handlebars, the faint island dawn light waking up the silver. A canvas pouch stuffed with folded newspapers hung over the front wheel.

Damon hawked and spit. "Okay then don't. But I tell you this—if you expect to take over this job, then you gotta find some guts. Or else if you don't, this place going *eat* you. And I talking more than dogs, little man."

Little man.

Damon had been calling him that a lot, lately. Boy didn't like it. And he didn't like the way Damon was always stepping in and telling him he had no guts. Damon needed to back off and give him a chance to prove he could take care of himself.

Damon pushed his bike ahead. "Gimme one paper," he said, yanking it out of Boy's bike bag.

He stood on his pedals and headed into the jungle. Boy watched Damon vanish around the curve, swallowed up by darkness.

Down that road of rocks and ruts was old man Cruz's place, an ancient shack of a house that got a paper. One measly paper. And Boy couldn't go there. Two weeks now and still he couldn't do it. Maybe Damon was right. Maybe he didn't have any guts.

Boy ducked when a bat buzzed his head. This time of day those things were all over the place.

He waited.

A few seconds later a rage of yapping and growling echoed through the trees and bushes. Jungle dogs. Or maybe it was just the dogs that lived at the Cruz house. Boy wiped his hand over his mouth, then squeezed his handgrips. He whipped his bike around so it faced the street, and glanced back over his shoulder to the dark road.

But he didn't run.

Damon came racing back. He spun a quarter-turn stop that sprayed pebbles and dirt over Boy's foot and clinked in his spokes. "Sooner or later you gotta face it, pantieboy."

Boy took off, heading down to the next street,

a street with lights, and Damon followed, shaking his head.

Forty minutes later, after all the papers had been delivered and the paper bag on Boy's bike flapped empty, they stopped to rest at the viewpoint between Kailua and Lanikai. From there you could see the long white beach that curled around the bay all the way down to the Marine Corps Air Station on the other side.

Damon sucked his teeth, then spit.

Boy squinted toward the sun, just now peeking its fiery eyes above the edge of the sea. On the beach below, a white-haired man dragged a small canoe into the ocean, then shoved it out, jumped aboard, and sat holding a paddle across the gunnels as it drifted toward the sunrise. It was a white canoe with a Hawaiian-style outrigger and it looked so peaceful out there on the glassy morning sea that Boy couldn't take his eyes off it.

"Let's go," Damon said.

"You go."

"What?"

Boy pointed his chin toward the ocean. "Look at that canoe."

Damon looked. "So?"

"You don't think it looks nice, on that smooth water?"

Damon frowned. "Shhh."

A car passed, its wind ruffling Damon's hair.

The radio was on. Loud, thumping bass. "How can you be my brother?" Damon said.

"What?"

"Sissyboy like you."

Boy stared at Damon, his glasses reflecting the fresh sun.

Damon shook his head and rode off.

2

DOWN ON THE BEACH a bird pecked in the sand, raising one foot when a small wave washed up and sailed under its belly. The wash slowed and stopped and slipped back out to sea and the wet sand it left behind reflected the pink of the sunrise. The bird went on pecking and Boy watched it until a larger wave made it fly into the ironwood trees that lined the beach.

The white-haired man was paddling toward the flat island that lay a short distance offshore. Boy watched him a moment, then hid his bike in the weeds and started down the rocky trail to the sand below.

Near the bottom he stepped on something that moved. He gasped and staggered back. A man wrapped in a sand-colored blanket bolted up. He had no shirt on and his shorts were greasy and his matted black hair stuck out like a beat-up old broom. "Hey!" the guy yelled. "Get outta here!"

6

"I'm sorry, I'm sorry," Boy said.

He crept around the man. Boy had seen him before, bumming around all over town. Boy ran toward the tracks left in the sand by the canoe when it was dragged to the water. He glanced back. The broom-haired man had gone back to sleep, so Boy stopped and sat.

He took off his glasses and held them to the sky, then wiped them on his T-shirt and put them back on.

The white canoe slipped from view behind the flat island. Above and beyond, the sunrise glowed pink and gold and spread into the sky like a fan. Boy breathed in deep and let his breath out slowly. He picked up a handful of fine white sand and let it slip through his fingers, smiling at some wandering thought. Marianne was in it, and that was what made him smile.

Ten or more minutes passed before the canoe came around the back side of the island. The man paddled down the coast a ways, then turned and headed back toward where Boy sat on the beach.

As he approached, Boy stood and brushed the sand from his hands and shorts.

The white-haired man waved, so Boy waited until the canoe bumped up on shore.

"I saw you watching me," the man said.

He was old. He looked as old as Boy's grampa,

before he died, but stronger than Grampa, tough and muscular. His eyes were the smiling kind with creased skin that shot out toward his temples. Like Boy, he wore only shorts and a T-shirt.

The man smiled and added, "I also saw you run into Gilbert." He nodded toward the bluff.

Boy turned and glanced back. "I didn't see him."

"Drugs. Messed him up. But he's harmless. Grumpy, but harmless. Sometimes I give him food."

Boy looked over at the sleeping man.

"What's your name, boy?"

"Boy."

"Boy's your name?"

"It's really James, but my dad knew somebody named Boy and liked it."

The white-haired man raised his eyebrows. "Sounds good to me. Mines is Buzzy."

"Nice canoe," Boy said.

"You like that? I made it. In fact, I made it when I was a kid about your age. I had this thing so long I can't even believe it."

"You made it? Yourself?"

"Most of it. My papa helped me. You know, because I was small, yeah? Like you. You must be, what? Eight? Nine?"

"Twelve."

"Twelve?"

Boy looked down. "Well, I am."

"How come you not home getting ready for school?"

"I got a paper route. I just finished."

"Good. Good."

Boy crossed his arms and looked at his feet.

Buzzy said, "You live close around here?"

Boy turned and pointed with his chin toward where the swampy canal emptied into the bay.

Buzzy said, "Sunnovagun, you my neighbor." He shook his head in amazement, then started to drag his canoe up the sand. He did it in short jerks, one, two, three, grunting with each pull.

Boy, his arms still crossed, watched him tug. Finally he said, "Want some help?"

"No-no. My exercise, this. Keeps me young, yeah?" Buzzy stopped pulling and stretched to his full height. He flexed a ropy arm and grinned.

Boy grinned back.

"Maybe someday I give you a canoe ride," Buzzy said.

"Really?"

"Sure. How's about tomorrow?"

"Tomorrow? *Yeah.* What time?"

"Same as today. Six-thirty."

"I'll be here."

"Me too, if the Big Man says okay." He looked to the sky and made the sign of the cross over his chest. Then he smiled at Boy and made a shaka sign that said, See you later, brah.

Boy lifted his chin goodbye and headed back to where he'd left his bike. He skirted the grumpy man, who was sitting up, now, saying to nobody, "Check the barometer. Check the radar. What's the bearing?"

Boy hurried up the bluff.

When he got to the viewpoint, he looked back and saw that Buzzy had dragged the canoe up to an old house and was in the yard showering under a garden hose.

Boy looked around. The sun was up now, and the place didn't look so spooky. There weren't any dogs of any kind around, good or bad. There were only the sleepy houses and quiet streets and the wild green weeds and trees.

From where he stood, Boy could also see the street he hated, the one where Damon's friend Rick said jungle dogs had been seen, dogs that used to belong to people until they were abandoned or had been run off or ran away themselves and got together and formed a pack and went wild and came down out of the hills at night. There were twenty of them, Rick said. Maybe more, so watch out, they're dangerous.

They could kill you.

That was what Rick said.

They could kill.

3

BOY COASTED BETWEEN two squawking chickens into his dusty yard. He got off and leaned his bike against the side of the house.

It was a worn-out dirt-stained house shaped like a box, the kind that was built a couple of feet off the ground so the bugs and rats couldn't get in. But nobody told the bugs that. They went in anyway. The rats could get in if they wanted to, but if they did, they had to deal with Damon's cat, Zorro, who Damon named after the guy in the old-time black-and-white TV show. Damon liked cats. He didn't like people very much, but he liked cats.

Toward the back of the house a swarm of flies hummed and swirled jagged patterns around two overstuffed garbage cans. Damon had forgotten to take them out to the street for the garbage truck. Right, Boy thought. He probably forgot because they were too heavy. If it was Daddy, he could take them both at one time, one in each hand.

Boy started back around to the front of the house when somebody yelled, "Hey!"

The screen door slapped open and Damon came out and down the three wood steps. Dressed in black, as always. Black bandanna over his hair, black T-shirt, black pants with a razor-sharp crease and a silver chain that hung from his belt loop to his wallet, which only had one thing in it: a fake ID that said he was twenty-one. With his shiny black shoes he kicked a rusty can that flipped and spun and clanked against the truck in the yard. Daddy's truck.

Boy watched Damon hunch away. He was short, like Mama. But he was scrappy.

The screen door whapped open again and Daddy stood filling the doorway. "I said *hey*!"

Without even bothering to glance back, Damon spit, "I going wear what I want, fat old man. I don't care *what* you say."

What was his *problem*? Boy thought. How come he had such a chip on his shoulder? Boy could remember how he used to puff out his chest when he followed Damon to the canal with his fishing pole. Damon was it, the king of all the guys he knew. It was nice. Back then he and Damon were friends.

Damon wasn't afraid of dogs, or scary guys, or

even Daddy. When Boy was really small, Daddy had seemed huge. Daddy was usually pretty quiet, though, except when he got mad, which wasn't very often. But when he did, you could probably hear him two miles away.

Damon was the king, all right. Back then. Now was different.

Daddy slammed his palm against the door frame, shaking the whole house. He noticed Boy and said, "Get in here. You're late and I ain't waiting around to drive you to school."

Boy lowered his eyes and walked up the steps past Daddy. It wasn't the first time Daddy and Damon had gotten into it over Damon's gang clothes.

Mama was at the sink, staring out the window into the backyard with her hands under running water, keeping quiet until everybody cooled off. Her black hair was tangled and she still wore the old T-shirt and boxer shorts that she'd slept in. A soft pink hibiscus sat in a jam jar on the window-sill. No screen. Everything was open to the warm air and the flies and the chatter of mynah birds.

Behind her Mike and Jason, the four-year-old twins, sat at the kitchen table, pushing and shoving each other, and making a lot of noise.

"Shuddup!" Daddy yelled.

Boy and the twins froze. They waited.

Mama turned off the water and reached for a

dish towel. When she saw Boy, she gave him a small, quick smile.

The twins gaped up at Daddy.

Daddy ran his hand over his face and took a deep breath. Then he bent down and kissed their heads and patted their backs and whispered, "Go on, eat your cereal. Go."

He stood and rubbed the back of his neck, and when he saw Boy watching him, he nodded for him to go get ready for school.

Boy went.

He passed Venita in the hall. She was seventeen, the oldest, and she was dressed in tight jeans and a white tank top with a gold chain hanging from her neck. On the chain was a guy's class ring, a guy named Herbie, who Damon called Slime. He graduated last year and got a job at a car wash. Damon said Slime even worked there, sometimes. Boy had never met him. He'd never come to the house.

Venita didn't look at Boy when they passed.

In his room—his and Damon's—Boy put on a pair of jeans and combed his hair with his fingers.

He noticed a black blob near Damon's pillow. Zorro, the cat, lazy as a lump. When Boy sat on Damon's bed, Zorro peeked open his slitty green eyes. "Working hard?" Boy said. Zorro closed his eyes and went back to sleep.

Boy's drawing journal was next to his alarm

clock on the concrete-block-and-plank shelf between his bed and Damon's. He picked it up and flipped it open to the last page he'd drawn on. There was a dog's head with mad red eyes and fangs and drops of blood dripping from its chin; a German army tank with a British fighter diving at it, shooting flames and bullets; a half-setting sun with rays shooting up; and five cubes. He was always drawing cubes, like three-dimensional boxes. Cubes and dog heads. He hated dogs. He didn't want to hate them, but he did because of a pit bull that scared him so bad one time that he actually made shi-shi in his pants.

He was about six years old, back when they lived in Kaneohe. Parts of his memory were ice clear, but some parts weren't. It had happened so fast.

He was walking down a dirt road to his friend Kenny's house when he passed somebody's yard. It had an old, loose chain-link fence around it. He could remember the day, clear and sunny. So nice. Then—

Wham! Bam!

The pit bull raced up and slammed into the fence, and the fence bowed out and hit Boy's arm and he could smell the stink of the dog and feel its hot breath in his ear and hear the snarling and snapping so near his face, about to break through and rip his heart right out of his chest. He stum-

bled back, and that's when he wet his pants. *Bam!*
Bam! Bam! The dog hit the fence. It wanted to *kill*
him. Boy staggered up and looked into the yard at
the wild-eyed dog, and beyond the dog there was
a rusted old car with no wheels, sitting in the
weeds. He could still see that car, like a dead
body, and that's how Boy remembered that day,
as the day he could have been dead, too.

He *hated* dogs. *Hated* them.

Boy looked up when he heard the front door
slap. Daddy taking Venita to school. He put the
journal back on the shelf and waited until he
heard the truck start up and the popping of tires
on the dirt-and-gravel driveway.

After Daddy drove off, Boy went out.

Mama turned the radio on to golden oldies.

The twins started up again and Boy scruffed
their hair, then grabbed a banana and kissed
Mama goodbye.

"Wait," she said, and got a comb she kept in a
jar by the sink. She filled the jar with water and
got the comb wet and Boy stood while she
combed his hair, the way she'd done all his life,
water dripping down his temples and soaking the
neck of his T-shirt.

She stood back and put her hand on his
cheek. "Watch out for cars."

Boy nodded and rubbed his face dry with the
heel of his hand.

Daddy wouldn't let him ride his bike to school because he was sure it would get stolen, so Boy had to walk, which was why he was almost always late. Three miles. First down Kailua Road, lined with ironwood trees, then down Kainalu Street and past the nice houses that had grass that was green and cars tucked in neat garages.

And he had to pass the high school, where Damon went, which was just before his own school. Small gangs of guys hung around outside before school started, and sometimes they waited for easy-money seventh-graders like him.

But no one would bother Boy, because of Damon.

For as long as Boy could remember, Damon had always watched out for him, even if Boy didn't like it.

It all started with Daddy, because of how Boy used to be afraid when Daddy lost his temper and shouted and banged his fist on the wall. When that happened, Boy hid under his bed.

Damon would crawl under there to get him out, saying, "Don't worry, it's okay. He just likes to make noise."

But now, Damon stepped in and tried to run Boy's fights for himself, for face, for his rep. And Boy wanted him to stop it. But how could he tell Damon that? He didn't want to get into another fight with him. One in a lifetime was enough.

4

HE WAS LATE.

Ms. Ching sighed and told him to go to his seat, then turned back to the chalkboard.

Gabriel Moto glared at Boy as he made his way to his desk. For some reason unknown to Boy, the two of them had never liked each other, all the way back from fifth grade, when it started. And now Gabriel hated Boy's guts even more because of how a couple of weeks ago when he was bothering Boy in the field after school, Damon came over and roughed Gabriel up. He said, "Next time I catch you messing with my brother, you going have a problem, man, a big, bad problem. With *me.*"

Why did Damon have to butt in like that?

Boy hurried to his seat with his head down.

On the chalkboard Ms. Ching wrote: *I look up to* ——— *because* ———.

Gabriel and his doofy friend Moose both

snickered when they read it. Boy noticed that almost all the girls sat with their mouths half open, probably mesmerized by Ms. Ching's perfect flowery script.

He glanced over at his friend Zeke, and Zeke nodded, and behind him Gabriel glared at Boy, slowly grinding his fist into his hand.

Boy reached into his desk and found his pencil and a piece of paper. He had a small stack of clean drawing paper hidden in there. He started drawing a cube.

Ms. Ching said, "Today we're going to talk about important people in our lives, people we look up to as models for our own lives. It might be someone in your family, or a friend, or even someone you don't know but admire. Can anyone think of anyone they look up to? And tell me why, too."

Eleven hands went up.

"Gabriel?"

"Evander Holyfield."

"Who?"

"And Van Damme."

"Hmmm, well, okay. Who else? And also tell me *why* you look up to these people."

No hands went up.

Somebody's book fell to the floor. Marianne Gomes, who sat across the aisle from Boy, reached down and picked it up. Her face was red, but her hair was as clean and shiny as polished black coral.

Boy looked at her until Ms. Ching said, "Okay then, let's go back to Gabriel. Gabriel, why do you look up to Van Damme?"

Gabriel slid down in his seat so far that the back of his neck hit the back of his chair. Without looking at Ms. Ching, he said, "Because he can beat you up?"

"So you look up to somebody who can beat people up?"

Gabriel mashed a small piece of paper with his fingers, then opened it back up and started tearing it into tiny strips. "Yeah," he said.

Moose added, "Because Van Damme always wins."

"For sure," Gabriel said, looking up for the first time.

Boy finished drawing the cube and started in on a dog's head. He started with the mouth, open and full of fangs—sharp, mean, throat-ripping, blood-dripping fangs.

He glanced up when the room got quiet.

Ms. Ching was pacing slowly, with a finger to her lips. "Okay," she finally said. "So someone who fights and wins is someone we can look up to. Does anyone disagree with that?"

Rose, who sat in front of Boy, raised her hand.

Her long dark hair sometimes fell back on Boy's desk. "I don't think anyone should look up to people who fight. I think it should be somebody nice, somebody who is good."

Others stepped in.

"Somebody who is honest."

"And smart."

"Somebody big, a big guy," Boy blurted out, then looked around to see if anyone was looking at him. Gabriel was. He held up a piece of paper with *Four eyes* written on it. Boy scowled at him, then turned back just as Marianne said, "Big *guy*? What about girls?"

"*Girls?*" Moose said. "How can anyone look up to a girl? That is so, so stupid."

Marianne burned Moose with her eyes, and when Moose turned away, she burned Boy.

Boy looked down at the dog head, sorry he'd said anything.

"Okay, okay," Ms. Ching said. "I've got you thinking, anyway." She crossed her arms and slowly walked to the other side of the room saying, "I have a couple of people I look up to. One is my brother Joey, who is deaf and has learned to read lips and talk almost as well as I can. There's also another person I look up to. *And,*" she added, dipping her head toward Marianne, "she's a woman."

Some of the boys snickered and shifted in their seats.

Boy stuck his chewed-up pencil between his teeth. A spitwad hit the back of his head and he whipped around. Gabriel grinned.

It was times like this that Boy dreamed he was as big and tough as Daddy. He could see it all in his mind—Gabriel would come looking for trouble and try to start a fight, and Boy would just stand there waiting, and that would make Gabriel mad, and Gabriel would throw a punch and Boy would catch his fist in his hand and twist and Gabriel would fall over crying, Ow! Ow! Ow! Boy thought maybe he might draw a picture of it.

Yeah, Boy thought. Gabriel would think twice before he messed with *me.*

Ms. Ching said, "You see, class, sometimes those we look up to aren't the people everybody knows. I admire people who face their challenges and overcome them with hard work, determination, and integrity. Of course they might have other qualities, too, but these are the ones that mean the most to me. Does that make sense?"

The class mumbled, "Yeah."

"Has anyone heard of a young woman named Heather Whitestone?"

Rose flapped her hand in the air, as excited as somebody's nervous Chihuahua. "I know, I know—Miss America."

Moose laughed. "Rose, you are so screwed up I can't even believe it."

Boy added ears and a neck to the dog head, then a back with rising fur. Then he started in on a human head, facing the fangs.

"That's *right*, Rose," Ms. Ching said. "Moose, come up here a minute. I want to tell you about Heather Whitestone."

Gabriel pointed at Moose and held his stomach and made big silent laughing motions. Moose pushed himself up and slouched to the front of the room.

Boy looked over at Zeke and grinned. Zeke was one of only three white guys in the class.

"Have you ever watched the Miss America pageant on TV, Moose?" Ms. Ching asked. Moose mumbled, "No," and Gabriel laughed out loud. Even Ms. Ching did, though she tried not to.

"Well, a few years ago a young woman named Heather Whitestone won it, and part of what she did to win was dance. She was incredible, Moose. Rose, can you tell Moose and the rest of us why it was so beautiful?"

Rose said, "Because she's deaf."

"Not," Gabriel said. "You can't dance if you're deaf."

"Yes you can, Gabriel," Ms. Ching said. "Heather heard that music through the vibrations in her feet."

Rose turned to Gabriel and smirked. Gabriel ignored her.

"Heather is not someone I look up to because she won a contest. I admire her because she had a *dream*. And despite tremendous odds, she made her dream come true."

Boy went back to the human head. He drew a mouth that was screaming and eyes that were popping out and hair that stuck up in fright, and then he put sweat drops splashing off the cheeks. Under the head he wrote, *Gabriel Moto begs for mercy*.

Ms. Ching said, "Moose, you can go back to your seat now," and he did, much faster than when he went up there. His chair screeched on the tile floor when he sat down. Gabriel stuck out his fist and Moose grinned and tapped it with his own.

Ms. Ching pointed to what she'd written on the chalkboard and said, "Now listen. I want you to think of someone you look up to, and I want you to write a short essay about that person. What's most important is that you think about *why* this person is admirable. In what way does he or she stand above the crowd? I'm assigning this because I think it's important that each of us has someone to look up to, someone to model our own life after. One page will do. I want it by

Wednesday next week. That's ten days, lots of time."

The class moaned and shuffled and grumbled like it was the worst, hardest, most unfair assignment Ms. Ching had ever given. But they did that every time she asked them to do something that sounded like work.

"Take out a piece of paper and write this down," she said, pointing to the chalkboard. "I'll give you ten minutes to get started. You can finish it at home. Remember, you have more than a week."

Most of the class started copying what was on the board and when Gabriel and Moose saw everybody writing, they started writing, too, making a big show of how much they were being put out.

Boy drew another cube, then bit his pencil and stared blank-eyed at the chalkboard.

Ms. Ching paced slowly down the aisles. She smiled when someone looked up, and when she saw Boy looking stumped, she nodded that he, too, should start writing. Boy bent over and pretended to write, shielding the dog and human head with his hands.

After Ms. Ching walked by, he put the drawing away and dug out a fresh piece of blue-lined, three-hole paper. At the top he wrote: *I look up to* ———— *because* ————. Then he got up and sharpened his mangled pencil.

When he got back to his seat, he sat staring at all the blank space on the paper. All the blank lines that had to be filled.

A spitwad landed on his desk. He flicked it off with his finger. Idiot Gabriel.

5

ON THE WAY HOME from school Boy saw Damon and the Cudas over in the beach park across from his street. They were in the shade of an ironwood tree in the empty parking lot, huddled around something.

There were only four Cudas now because Zippy moved to Honolulu and Masa was on probation for scratching up somebody's car with a key. So now there was Damon, Bobby, Joker, and Rick. Only stupid people messed with them.

Bobby was kneeling down doing something.

Boy pushed his glasses up with his thumb and walked over with his math book and the blank essay paper between the pages.

Joker said, loud enough for Boy to hear, "Hey, Damon, here comes your sister," which Boy had heard so many times that he didn't even care anymore.

Damon, still in black but shirtless, glanced over his shoulder at Boy, then looked back down at Bobby.

Boy stood a little ways back from the Cudas. But he could see what they had. A chicken. "What are you doing?" he said.

The Cudas ignored him. He wasn't even there.

Boy crouched to see better.

With one hand Bobby held the chicken pressed to the pavement with its neck stretched out like he was going to cut its head off. With his other hand he pulled a piece of white chalk out of his pocket and drew a line on the pavement, straight out from the chicken's beak. The chicken's eyes crossed. Then they glazed over. Then froze.

Bobby let go.

The chicken didn't move.

It looked like a pile of feathers, or a dust mop. Boy squinted and studied its eyes, which didn't even blink.

Rick said to Bobby, "You *killed* it."

Bobby picked up the chicken and held it in his hand like a sleeping cat. It didn't flick a feather. It didn't squawk. It didn't do anything. Bobby handed it to Rick and Rick winced and held it gently out in front of him in two hands. "What do I do with it?"

"Whatever you want. It's hypnotized."

"Hypnotized." Rick's eyes grew wide, which was unusual since Rick was the meanest of the Cudas and everybody just assumed he'd seen it all, done it all, and knew it all. He could twist the head off that chicken in a flash. But he held the chicken like something about it scared him.

He handed it back to Bobby.

"Make it come back to life," Rick said.

"Why?"

"It's too weird, man. Make it come back."

Bobby lifted the chicken up and gazed into its frozen eyes. "It *is* weird, ain't it?"

"Give it here."

Joker took the chicken, then reached it out to Boy. "Hold this a minute," he said.

Boy put his math book down on the pavement and took the chicken.

"Be real careful now," Joker said. "Don't hurt it."

Joker tapped Boy on the arm and they all started to leave, laughing at Boy standing there staring at the bird.

"Hey," Boy said. "What do I do with it?"

"Fry it up for dinner," Bobby said, and they all laughed.

But they stopped laughing when they saw the truck, a cherry-red Chevy pickup with flashy chrome wheels. It crept into the parking lot, engine rumbling low.

The Cudas watched it drive up. Nobody moved.

The truck turned in front of Joker, nearly bumping him. It stopped and Joker stepped back.

Seven killer-eyed guys. Three in front. Four in back.

The truck idled a moment, then shut down. The place fell silent, except for the waves out on the beach.

The driver looked the Cudas over.

Crowboy.

Who got his name by creaming somebody with a crowbar. And who was Gabriel Moto's older brother.

The sound of small waves *whoomped* on the sand.

Whoomp.

Whoomp.

If Damon and the Cudas were worried, they didn't show it, all of them as hard-eyed as the truck guys.

Crowboy opened the door and turned to face them, sitting sideways in the seat. But he didn't get out. He stared at Damon, all the while slowly pulling a cigarette out of a pack from his shirt pocket, sticking it between his lips, striking a match and lighting it. Shaking the match out.

Nobody else moved. Nobody spoke.

Crowboy took a long drag and flicked the

match at the Cudas. It hit Rick and fell to the ground. Rick didn't even blink.

Crowboy glared at Damon. "Which one of you dead boys was giving my brother trouble?"

Boy slowly stepped back, still holding the lifeless chicken.

"Who's your brother?" Damon finally said.

Crowboy snickered. He eased out of the truck and all the other guys jumped out after him and slowly walked around the Cudas.

Crowboy came up and stood in Damon's face, looking down on him. But Damon didn't flinch, even though Crowboy had a rep as long as his leg, a bad rep. Twelfth grade. Damon was ninth.

"You know who's my brother," Crowboy said. "But in case you forgot, I going remind you. He's in that punk's class." He tipped his head toward Boy.

Crowboy took another pull on his cigarette, then blew out a slow stream of smoke around his words. "Was you, yeah? Messing with my brother."

Boy's eyes were popped open like a bottom fish. Damon wasn't going to back down. Boy thought, Come on, Damon, don't be stupid. Don't make him mad.

Crowboy shoved Damon lightly. Damon stepped back, but he didn't fall.

"How come you got all black clothes on?"

Crowboy said. "Am I supposed to be scared of you?"

The six other ice-eyes moved closer to the Cudas, who looked kind of puny now.

Then Crowboy noticed Boy holding the chicken.

He stuck his cigarette in his lips and it flapped when he said, "What's that?"

Boy mumbled, "A chicken."

"What?"

"A chicken," he said louder.

"Of course it's a chicken. You think I'm stupid? Is it dead or what?"

"It's hypnotized."

"Naah," Crowboy said, acting now as if he'd forgotten all about Gabriel's problems. But Boy knew he hadn't. Oh no.

"Make it do something then," Crowboy said.

Boy looked at Bobby.

Bobby waited a second, then came over and took the chicken from Boy. He shook it. The chicken awoke, squawked, and nipped Bobby's arm. Bobby dropped it and it scurried away screeching.

Crowboy laughed. "How you did that?"

"With a chalk."

"No kidding, a chalk. That's cool, man."

Crowboy sounded almost friendly, but Boy knew he wasn't.

Crowboy stuck his hand under his T-shirt and scratched his chest. A small tattoo of a knife dripping blood cut across the side of his flat stomach. "If one of you punks bothers my brother one more time, I going make you wish you was dead, yeah? You going wish you was floating in the canal . . . with the garbage."

He stared at Damon.

And Damon blinked. Boy saw it.

Crowboy turned to Boy. "You must be a pretty tough midget to run around with these stupits. Is that right? You tough?"

"No," Boy whispered.

Crowboy poked Boy's chest with his finger. "My brother don't like you. Every time you call your brother when you got problems. Maybe Gabriel going beef with you, yeah. He never beefed no midget before."

"I don't call my brother," Boy whispered, staring at Crowboy's chest. Anywhere but his eyes.

"Oh yeah? That's not what I heard."

"Well, you heard wrong."

Crowboy cracked a grin. He had a missing front tooth that somebody probably kicked down his throat. He reached out and pinched Boy's cheek.

"*Ow!*" Boy jerked back. A red bruise rose quickly.

"That's for your smart mouth," Crowboy said.

Instantly Damon was on Crowboy and just as fast Crowboy had Damon's neck in the crook of his arm, squeezing. "You like go in the canal right now, little fut?"

Damon slashed at Crowboy with his fists but stopped when Crowboy squeezed harder. Damon's face turned red and a vein on his forehead popped up. The Cudas didn't step in to help, not with all those guys around them.

Crowboy gave Damon's neck a twist, then shoved him away.

Damon gasped and grabbed his throat.

Slowly the truck guys backed away and climbed into the pickup and cruised out of the parking lot in the same crawling way they'd come in.

When they were gone, Damon went up to Boy and spit on his shirt. Boy jumped back.

"You *coward*! You just stand there and let him *shame* you?"

Boy looked away, his eyes starting to water, the pinch on his cheek bloodred. Crowboy *had* scared him. But he hadn't asked Damon to step in.

Damon shouted in his face, "You gotta get some *guts!*" He rubbed his throat and coughed and the Cudas walked away.

When they were gone, Boy took off his glasses and rubbed a knuckle over his eyes, then picked up his math book with the paper stuck in it. He started home with a stinging welt on his cheek as bright and hot as a grease burn.

But what hurt the most was the spit on his shirt.

6

BOY SAT ALONE at the kitchen table picking at his dinner of cold leftover tuna casserole, toast, and a glass of milk. Above, three dusty moths sat on the lightbulb that hung from the ceiling, and he could smell the faint odor of their roasting wings.

Mama was outside trying to stuff more garbage into the garbage cans. Daddy lay stretched out on the couch watching *Monday Night Football* with his dinner plate on his belly. Mike and Jason sat cross-legged on the ragged carpet below him, their mouths and fingers gleaming with buttery toast. Zorro crouched nearby, waiting for one of them to drop something. Venita was in her room on the phone with Slime. Damon hadn't come home at all.

"Get 'um, get 'um!" Daddy yelled at the TV. "Shee!"

The back door squeaked open and Mama came in and washed her hands at the sink. Now her hair was clean and combed and she was wearing shorts and a new T-shirt and thin rubber slippers. She turned off the tap and shook the water from her hands. "What happened to your cheek?" she said, picking up the dish towel. "It's all red."

Boy touched the bruise. "Uh . . . at school . . . I got hit by a baseball."

"Ouch! Does it hurt?"

"A little."

Mike and Jason were making too much noise. Daddy yelled, "Go play somewheres else! I can't hear the TV!"

Mama glanced over at him and shook her head. Then, to Boy, she said, "You have any homework tonight?"

"Yeah."

"What is it?"

"Just something I gotta write."

Mama put down the dish towel. "Well, what do you have to write?"

Boy looked at his plate.

Mama walked over and put her hand on Boy's back. "I'm just interested in what you're doing, that's all."

Boy pushed the plate away. "Okay . . . I gotta tell about someone I look up to." He peeked up at Mama.

"Who's it gonna be?"

Boy shrugged. "I don't know."

Mama crossed her arms and scrunched her eyes. "Hmmm . . . Why don't you ask Daddy?"

Boy looked toward the couch just as Daddy yelled, "He's gonna pass, watch it, watch it . . . aw man, *jeese*! He was wide open!" He took his plate off his belly and put it on the coffee table. He groaned up and hovered over the TV to turn up the volume because of all the noise Mike and Jason were making.

"Yeah, maybe he'd know somebody," Boy said. "But I gotta tell why, too."

"Why what?"

"Why I look up to him . . . or her."

Mama tipped her head toward the TV and said, "Daddy would know." She tapped Boy's back. "But *you* can think of somebody."

Just then the phone rang. Half a ring.

"Mom!" Venita yelled from her bedroom. "It's Auntie Irma."

Mama picked up the phone in the kitchen. "Sissy," she said. Mama still called her that, left over from when she was small and Auntie Irma was her big sister.

Boy frowned. Who could he look up to?

"Saturday's fine," Mama said. "We're not going anywhere. So how does it look, the bracelet?"

Boy drew a cube. A nice one, three-dimensional.

Mama said, "How's Andy doing? Still like Oregon?"

Boy peeked up when he heard *Andy,* who was his cousin. Boy liked him a lot. He played baseball at Oregon State.

Mama hung up and said, "Andy's got a girl-friend."

Boy grinned. Andy always was a lover boy. "What's her name?"

"Emily."

"Hah!" Boy said. "Same as you."

Mama shook her head and said, "That boy."

At eight-thirty Mama put Mike and Jason to bed, and since their room was right by the TV set, she made Daddy go out and listen to the rest of the game in his truck, like always. He never seemed to mind.

The phone rang, and Venita shouted, "I'll get it."

Boy sat with his chin resting on his palm, staring at a newspaper photo of Mama's best friend, Rita, taped to the refrigerator. She was standing by a painting of two kids on a beach with a dog, and underneath the photo it talked about how Rita worked for the police department in Kailua. She and Mama had been friends since second grade. Both of them had married their high-school sweethearts, as Mama called Daddy. Rita was almost pure Hawaiian.

Mama had the blood, too. She was mostly Hawaiian, but also had Chinese, a little Filipino, and even some Portuguese, like Daddy.

Mama was usually a happy person. But she seemed kind of lonely now. It was probably because she missed Gramma and Grampa Makuakane, her parents, who had retired and moved to Las Vegas. Boy missed them, too, but he also felt good about Las Vegas, because someday he might visit them there.

Gramma Regis, Daddy's mama, was still around, though. And Mama loved her as much as she loved Gramma Makuakane. But Gramma Regis was old, now, and her mind was going.

Boy's thoughts drifted to Kaneohe, where Gramma and Grampa Regis lived. A long time back, before Grampa died, he and Damon used to go up to their house up in the banana groves almost every other weekend, and they would play like army guys, or sometimes pirates, stalking through the banana trees. Grampa even cut each of them a sword and a wooden rifle on his jigsaw. It was great, Boy thought. Him and Damon.

Boy rubbed his face and looked away from the article about Rita. He tapped his fingernails on his teeth. Who could he look up to? He wanted it to be someone in his family. But who? Maybe there was someone else.

He didn't feel like asking Daddy anything right now, not with the game on.

Except for what he'd copied at school, his paper was still blank. Which was still in his math book. Which was lying on his bed. He got up and rinsed his plate and went to his room to get it.

Venita finally got off the phone and came out of her room. She followed him back to the kitchen, singing, "*Un-break my heart, say you'll love me again.* . . . You like that song, James?" She always called him James, because she knew it irritated him.

Boy stopped and turned. "Are you talking to me?"

"Your name is *James,* isn't it?"

She brushed past him and took an apple and a half-empty can of Coke out of the refrigerator.

Boy sat back down at the kitchen table.

Venita leaned against the counter taking bird bites out of the apple, her long, smooth legs crossed at the ankles. She was wearing the blue knee-length T-shirt that she sometimes slept in. On the front was a silver star and *Dallas Cowboys* written in white below it. Venita's hair was dark brown and long. And she had green eyes, like Zorro.

She watched Boy stare at his blank paper.

Boy looked up. She smiled and he looked back down at his paper, then back up again.

"What's wrong with your face?" she asked.

"I got hit by a ball."

Venita raised an eyebrow.

Boy turned away.

Venita went back to her room. "*Un-cry these tears . . .*"

He drew a small cube. Then erased it.

Finally, he got up and took his book and his paper and his pencil outside and sat on the creaky wooden steps in the faint light coming from the house.

For a moment he listened to the football game, small and tinny in Daddy's truck. Daddy was in the cab with his head back and his eyes closed. In the back of the truck rakes, shovels, brooms, and hoes stood neat and tidy in their holders. There was also a lawn mower, a gas can, a wheelbarrow, a leaf blower, and a bunch of other junk that Daddy used to clean up people's yards.

Somebody's mangy German shepherd came nosing around out by the road. Boy watched it sniff every interesting spot in front of the house and around the dusty driveway before it moved on down the street.

Boy chewed on his pencil and stared at the

shadowy trees, then suddenly took the pencil out
of his mouth and wrote:

I look up to my dog.
Because . . .
Because . . . he saved my life.

SOMEBODY NUDGED HIM the next morning, before his alarm went off.

He bolted up. "What time is it?"

"Four-thirty."

The shadow that hovered over him moved and Boy could see that it was Daddy. "Where's Damon?" Boy asked.

"Not home. Let's go. We gotta get those papers delivered."

Daddy left.

Boy got up and found his glasses and turned the alarm off on his clock. He put on his shorts and a clean T-shirt and went into the bathroom and brushed his teeth in the dark. Before he went out to fold newspapers, he checked Damon's bed. Empty. The sheet was crumpled and crammed at the bottom just like it had been the night before. The black blob of Zorro was curled on the pillow.

Outside, there were no clouds and there were

still a few thousand stars in the sky and a small breeze whispered in the twisty hao trees down along the canal. There was a smell in the air like sulfur and dead fish, but not so strong that it stank. Except for the leaves and the faint rush of the ocean beyond, the silence was complete.

Out by the road Daddy bent over and picked up the bound stack of newspapers. He walked back under the pale green streetlight with his fingers hooked under the binding. Where was Damon? Boy didn't want to ask.

Daddy dropped the papers at the bottom of the steps and popped the binding with his pocketknife. Together, they folded and pounded the papers tight and made a small pile of them in the dirt around their feet.

When they were done, Boy started over to get his bike.

"Forget the bike," Daddy said. "Put 'um in the truck."

They put the papers in a cardboard box between them on the seat. The cab smelled like gas and grease and rotting grass mixed together. The seats were vinyl and shiny from use, and a silver crucifix hung from the rearview mirror. On the floor by Boy's feet was a pad of invoices printed with *Regis Landscaping* on the top.

Daddy backed the truck out with the lights off. When they got out on the road, he stopped and sat with the truck idling and his arm out the window. He leaned forward and looked up at the stars. "Nice, yeah?"

"What?"

"Stars out. Nobody around. Peaceful."

He looked at Boy. Boy had never heard Daddy say anything like that before.

Daddy grinned, and with his hand spread wide reached over and tapped Boy's chest twice. "Let's go do it, big guy."

Daddy drove, and Boy threw the papers into the driveways and yards of all the houses that got papers, all the time telling Daddy which streets to take, and Daddy did not once question any of Boy's directions.

When they turned into the Cruz place, Daddy stopped and peered into the dark jungle ahead. "I heard you scared of this place."

"Who said that?"

"Damon."

"Well, he's wrong."

"Good. Take this paper and walk it down to the house."

Boy took the paper. But he didn't get out.

"I thought you said you wasn't scared."

Daddy wasn't angry. Curious, maybe.

They sat.

Daddy said, "You like me to come with you?"

Boy looked at him. "Okay, but . . . but

there's wild dogs in there. Jungle dogs. And they could kill you.''

"Who told you that?''

"Damon's friend Rick.''

"Pshhh. You know who lives here?''

"Yeah. Old man Cruz.''

"Old man Cruz. Even when I was a small kid we called him old man Cruz. Nice guy. Long time in that house, long time. Always he had dogs. Loud, make lot of noise. I don't know how come Rick told you they could kill you. Crazy to say that. They might bite you if you look dangerous. But you don't look dangerous. Come on, let's go.''

"I'm not talking about *those* dogs. I'm talking about the *wild* ones.''

"Pshhh. Let's go.''

Boy got out and closed his door quietly.

Daddy thumped his shut.

Boy jumped.

A dog went off. Then another.

Daddy put his hand on Boy's shoulder and urged him forward. "You don't like this job, do you?''

"I like this job . . . just not this part of it.''

"That's okay. I don't like some parts of my job, either. But gotta do it anyway, yeah? Or else we all going starve.''

They walked down the road into the trees and around the long dark bend and beyond to a clearing where the house was. Boy peered into the jungle and thought about starving. He hadn't ever heard Daddy say something like that before, either. It was a strange thought.

Two dogs came running out, barking, snapping, growling, circling. But not biting. Not killing.

Daddy clicked his tongue, *"Tst tst tst,"* and the dogs quieted. "Good dogs," he whispered smooth as cream, "good boys," and the dogs wagged their tails and nudged him with their noses.

A gust of wind whipped up and swayed the trees. The stars were gone now and a cloudy haze was growing in the faint light of daybreak. Daddy smelled the air. "Rain coming."

Boy watched the clouds move across the treetops.

Daddy put his hand on Boy's shoulder and said, "Put that paper up by the house and let's go."

Boy did.

The dogs followed them all the way back to the truck.

They got in and Daddy started it up and backed it out to the street, looking through the rear window with his arm behind Boy. "Those dogs going come at you every time. So you gotta get them used to your smell, and your sound.

Click your tongue or snap your finger, something like that. Same thing every time. Pretty soon they come to know you. No need to be scared. Those dogs just doing their job, yeah? Just being dogs."

"But what about the wild ones? What if they come?"

Daddy stopped out on the street and shifted into first, the gears complaining. "I don't believe what Damon's friend told you," he said.

"How come you don't believe it?"

"What?"

"About the wild dogs. How come you don't believe it?"

"If there was killer dogs around here, everybody would know about it. Believe me, everybody would know."

They drove around the viewpoint and down into Lanikai delivering papers, and after a while Boy said, "But still they could be real."

"Who could be real?"

"The jungle dogs, the wild ones."

Daddy looked over at him. "You still worrying about that?"

"No," Boy said, his voice trailing off.

Daddy reached over and scruffed Boy's hair. "That's okay. When I was a kid, I was scared of things, too."

"Like what?"

"Snakes."

"We don't have snakes here."

"I know. But I was scared of them anyway."

By then the sun was up, but it was covered by a gray haze that grew into long, high clouds, and in the air a gusting wind kicked up sand and dust along the sides of the road. When they drove back over the viewpoint, Boy looked out over a sea scarred by whitecaps.

"Can I get out here?"

Daddy pulled over and stopped. "You want to get out in *this* weather?"

"I want to walk back on the beach," Boy said, studying the ocean. Would Buzzy even think of going out on a day like this? "I still have plenty of time before school."

Daddy put his hand to Boy's chin and turned his face toward him. "How'd you get that bruise?"

"At school. A baseball."

Daddy frowned.

Boy got out, but before he shut the door, he said, "How come Damon was gone already this morning?"

Daddy looked at him a moment. "He never came home, son."

"Why?"

"He's mad at me."

"For what?"

"Just about anything you can think of, seems like." Daddy smiled, kind of sad.

Boy stared back at him. Where could Damon be? He closed the door.

Daddy said, "You ain't mad at me, too, are you?"

"No."

Daddy grinned and gave him a thumbs-up and drove off.

The wind swirled dust off the road as Boy watched the truck grind down the hill. It vanished around the bend. He stood a moment longer, looking at where it had been.

8

THE WIND BLEW UP small blizzards of fine white sand that raced down the beach and stung his legs and feet. The rising gray-green sea wasn't yet a red-flag sea, or dangerous, but it wasn't welcoming.

Boy turned when a gust wheezed in the ironwood trees behind him, bending the trees and pelting the beach with olive-size pinecones.

"Choppy today," Buzzy said.

Boy jumped. "*Jeese!* I didn't even see you come up."

"You were looking the other way."

Boy glanced back at the ironwoods rocking in the wind. "I kind of like stormy weather," he said.

"Me too." Buzzy found a bottle cap in the sand and flicked it out toward the water, but the wind blew it off to the side. "You ready?"

"It's too rough . . . isn't it?" Boy glanced at the windy sea. It might be exciting. Or stupid.

"Naah. Good like this. Get a little wet, but so what?"

Boy looked out toward the flat island with the water white and foamy around its shores. Farther down the bay, the rainbowed sail of a windsurfer flew toward them at what looked like thirty or forty miles an hour.

"The Osborn kid," Buzzy said. "He's good. Real good. And strong as an eel. He lives for wind like this."

The windsurfer dipped and dodged and leaped the choppy swells and Buzzy said, "Man, I wish I could do that. Probably break my back. But you could do it, you practice a little." Then he said, "Come. Let's get the canoe."

The wind grabbed Boy's glasses and almost blew them off, so he held them in place as he walked up to Buzzy's yard.

Gilbert, the scary man, was sitting cross-legged on the grass with his hands around a steaming cup. When he saw Buzzy, he said, "The four planets of navigation are Venus, Mars, Jupiter, and Saturn. They are easily identifiable, and when visible, provide good sights." Then he turned and stared off in the other direction.

"I gave him some coffee," Buzzy said.

"What . . . What did he just say?"

"He's just babbling. He's a smart guy, in a way. Talks a lot about survival at sea, for some reason.

And boats, what he reads in the library. If I try to talk to him, he shuts up, like now. Sometimes he stops right in the middle of what he's saying, and that's it. Pau for the day. Done." Buzzy shook his head. "Sad, yeah?"

Gilbert wouldn't look at Boy or Buzzy. Just the ocean. What was he thinking?

"Let's get this thing in the water," Buzzy said, and they hauled the canoe down across the beach.

Within minutes they were paddling into the chop.

Boy sat in front and Buzzy in back, guiding the canoe toward the island. The Osborn kid whipped past, grinning like crazy, and Buzzy raised his paddle. Boy watched the taut sail dip and dodge and saw the kid's bulging back muscles. The sail hummed and snapped in the wind. How free that kid must feel!

When they got to the island, Boy was soaked head to foot and his arms were rubber. Jeese, Buzzy was tough.

They had to paddle hard to make headway. They rounded the back side of the island, which Boy now saw for the first time, the rugged coral rim and the snarling churn of waves along its edge. Beyond was the grayish island of Oahu, its mountains now hazed in a veil of rain.

They worked their way down the coast toward

the marine base, then turned and headed back. The wind raised bumps on Boy's skin. When they got back to shore, they pulled the canoe out of the water and up into Buzzy's yard. They fell to the grass and sat. Boy took off his glasses and wiped them on his soaked shirt. He squinted, looking for Gilbert. But Gilbert was gone.

Boy put his glasses back on, smiling. He felt warm inside, and tired. He nodded to Buzzy. Then they looked back at the windy sea.

9

HE WAS LATE. AGAIN.

But Ms. Ching had her back to the class and Boy slipped in.

Gabriel threw a spitwad at him, but it missed and landed in Rose's hair. She reached back and took the wet thing out. She dropped it and turned around to glare at Boy.

Boy thumbed back at Gabriel, who sat looking innocent.

Rose scowled at both of them.

When she turned back, Gabriel laughed silently, his shoulders shaking.

Boy wiped the rain off his math book and checked inside to see if his essay was still there.

"Good morning, Mr. Regis," Ms. Ching said. "Do we need to buy you an alarm clock?"

"No," Boy mumbled, without looking up.

"Okay, class," Ms. Ching said, "let's get to

work. It's science day. But first, how are you doing on your essays? Does anyone have anything started yet?''

Without looking into his desk, Boy reached in and pulled out the paper with the dog head and Gabriel's head on it. He found his pencil.

Rose raised her hand.

"Wonderful, Rose," Ms. Ching said. "Can we hear what you've written so far?''

Rose stood. *"I look up to Heather Whitestone because she became Miss America. She is deaf and she still became Miss America. I believe this is a great thing and this is why I look up to her."*

Rose sat back down.

Ms. Ching put her hands in the pockets of her skirt. "That's nice, Rose, but . . . but I'd like you to try to come up with someone we haven't talked about. Think of someone close to *you.* Someone in your family, maybe, or someone you know, or someone you may not know but admire."

Rose stared at her desk.

Boy shielded his drawing and started adding a snake. A cobra with an open throat and monster fangs, coming at Gabriel from behind.

"Who else brought something?''

The rain tapped on the windows.

"Nobody?''

Boy stopped drawing. He covered the snake and dog-head paper with his book, then slowly raised his hand.

"Thank you, Boy," Ms. Ching said.

Boy took out the folded paper and opened it up. *"I look up to my dog—"*

The whole class broke out laughing, roared, like they'd been starved for a month for something to laugh about.

They turned around in their seats and gaped at him and a wave of some horrible sickly feeling surged through him like a nightmare.

He kept his eyes on the paper.

"Stop this *instant*!" Ms. Ching shouted.

She faced the class with a pair of clenched fists, and the class settled down. She glared at each one of them, one after the other. "You should be *ashamed* of yourselves. Except for Rose and Boy, not *one* of you had the courage to step up and share your work. Now I want each of you to give Boy the respect of listening. . . . Do you hear me?"

Silence.

"All right," she said. "Go on, Boy."

Boy shifted the paper from one hand to the other, then held it in both hands. *"I look up to . . . I look up to . . ."*

"It's okay, Boy," Ms. Ching said. "We all want to hear what you have to say."

Boy took a breath, then started again. *"I look up to my dog, Pilot, because he saved my life."*

He stopped and looked up. Ms. Ching nodded to go on.

"I . . . I took him over the ridge into Bellows Field and we were attacked by a pack of jungle dogs. My dog got into a fight with two of them and won and the others ran away. His neck was ripped open and I had to carry him home. When we got there we had to take him to the vet. But he died before we got there."

Boy stopped reading. Everyone waited.

Gabriel stared at Boy with his mouth slightly open.

Ms. Ching said, "That's amazing, Boy. See me after class, okay?"

Boy nodded and folded the paper.

After everyone left the room for recess, Ms. Ching came over to sit in Marianne's chair across from Boy. Boy looked at his desk where somebody had gouged LOVE into the wood with a ballpoint pen.

Yelling and the thumping sound of the tetherball and the clink and ring of its chain rushed in through the open windows.

Ms. Ching said, "What you wrote is very interesting, Boy. It's creative . . . and unusual."

Boy looked up, then back down.

"In fact," Ms. Ching added, "it's so good that I want you to add to it."

Boy nodded.

"This time see if you can remember more of the details. Maybe you could include how you felt when you first saw the dogs that attacked you. Or maybe you can remember what the air smelled like, or something about the heat or the dust and dirt. Little things like that will help us get a stronger sense of what it must have been like to have been there. Details can put real power into your essay."

Boy fingered years of scratched names and drawings all over his desktop.

"You surprised me today," Ms. Ching said.

Boy looked up.

Ms. Ching touched his arm. "You're usually so quiet."

Boy nodded. He knew what to add to the essay: the stickiness of blood, the fangs, the growling and ripping, the . . .

"Maybe a new Boy is waking up inside you," Ms. Ching said. "I like him."

Boy tried to look pleased.

10

THE FIELD BETWEEN the elementary school and the high school was wide and grassy. Now, after the wind and rain had passed, the clouds were open to the sun, and steam rose from the grass where Boy walked.

"Hey Boy!" somebody called. "Wait up!"

Boy stopped. It was his friend Zeke, a haole kid, a white boy whose dad was a commander in the U.S. Navy. He was kind of blubbery, and though he and Boy were the same age, Zeke looked at least a year older.

Zeke caught up and bent over with his hands on his knees, breathing hard. He said, "You want . . . to go over to . . . Bellows?"

"Are you crazy?"

Zeke stood, his chest still heaving. "Come on, I need more machine-gun shells. . . . You can get some, too."

"No way. You heard what I wrote. I ain't going there."

"Get outta here. You think I believe that?"

"Believe what?"

"That stupid lie you wrote."

Boy blinked. "It's true."

"Sure it is. Come on, if we start soon we can be back before five."

"It *is* true!"

"Boy, that story is so fake I can't believe it."

"It's *not* fake . . . but I'll go. But it's a stupid idea."

"Why?"

"Because there's wild dogs there."

Zeke shook his head.

"Well, there are. Rick said. And they could *kill* you."

"Rick's an idiot."

Boy scowled. "Okay, but if we see any dogs, I'm gone."

"Fine."

They were walking across the middle of the field when a small stone hit Boy in the back. *"Arf,"* someone barked.

Boy turned.

Gabriel.

And Moose, and one other guy, Barry.

They walked up and Gabriel said, "Hey, bottle

eyes, where's your dog?" Moose and Barry laughed.

"Leave him alone," Zeke said.

"Shut up, fats. I wasn't talking to you."

"You gonna make me?"

"Okay."

Fop!

Gabriel slugged Zeke in the gut. Zeke crumpled over, gasping. Boy tried to help him but Gabriel shoved him away, and Boy stumbled back and fell.

"Hey!" somebody yelled.

It was Damon and Bobby and Joker and Rick. "Get up," Damon said to Boy, his eyes fixed on Gabriel.

Boy and Zeke staggered up.

"I don't need you! Stay out of it! I can take care of this myself," Boy said to Damon. He didn't know if he could, but anything would be better than Damon stepping in and making it worse.

"Shuddup!" Damon said. Then, to Gabriel, "Didn't we already talk about this? I guess your mem'ry ain't so good, huh?"

Rick said, "Is *this* Crowboy's brother? Hey, you. Your brother's ugly and got a red truck?"

Gabriel said, "Yeah, and when I tell him you called him ugly, you better hide."

"I just thought of something," Damon said. He put his hand on Gabriel's shoulder and pulled him closer like he was going to tell him a secret. "How you going tell anybody anything when your face going be too broke to talk?"

Gabriel slapped Damon's hand away. Moose's eyes were wide and darting around and Barry took off.

"Wait wait wait," Moose said. "We weren't going to hurt anybody. We just fooling around, just joking, man."

Damon said, "Eh, fat boy, was they just joking?" Zeke shook his head.

Damon looked at Moose. "I guess you wrong, brah."

Moose pulled Gabriel back. "We don't need no beef with these guys."

"You got that right," Rick said. He whapped his fist out, snapping it back a half inch from Moose's face. Moose jerked back and his hands flew up.

Gabriel glared at Boy. "You and me going talk later. For sure, yeah?"

"Hey!" Damon said, grabbing Gabriel's shirt. "There ain't going be no later. What I gotta tell you, man? I can't believe you so deaf."

Gabriel slapped Damon's hand away again and spit at him. Damon hit him in the face.

"No!" Boy jumped forward as Gabriel staggered back and fell. Gabriel sat up and put his hand to his mouth, and spit some blood. "Before, I was just scaring you," he said to Boy. "But now I ain't."

Gabriel got up and walked away with Moose.

Damon turned to Boy and said, "I *told* you they going eat you. You ain't embarrassed?"

"I didn't need you!" Boy said. "Look what you did!"

Damon grinned and brushed his hand over Boy's T-shirt as if to remove some dirt. "Sorry, little man. You need help. I can't just let somebody mess up my own brother, yeah?"

The Cudas slouched away.

Boy and Zeke started walking toward Zeke's house.

Boy mashed his lips. It used to be so different. He and Damon did things together, like up at Gramma and Grampa's, like fishing in the canal. Good times. And Damon was always nice to him. Now look.

Zeke rubbed his stomach.

"Did it hurt?" Boy asked.

"Yeah."

"I'm sorry."

"For what?"

"It was my fault. Gabriel hates me, not you."

Zeke shrugged. "I don't think he likes anybody, really."

"Stupid Gabriel."

"I'd hate to be in Damon's shoes," Zeke said.

"Why?"

"Crowboy."

"Damon ain't afraid of him."

"He should be."

Boy nodded. "I know it."

11

ZEKE'S MOM WAS LOUNGING on the couch, one arm snaking along the back of it with a long white cigarette smoking between her fingers. She glanced over her shoulder when Zeke and Boy walked in. "Hi, honey," she said, then turned back to the TV.

Zeke didn't even look at her.

Boy wanted to say hi. It didn't feel right just to walk in and not say something. But he kept quiet. It didn't seem to bother anyone how Zeke was ignoring her.

Boy whispered to Zeke, "Where's your dad?"

"Somewhere between Mexico and the North Pole. Who knows?"

"When's he coming home?"

Zeke shrugged. "You like Oreos?"

"Sure I like Oreos."

They headed through the kitchen on their way to Zeke's room.

Zeke shut his door and locked it.

Boy *loved* Zeke's room, and he loved how Zeke could close the door and lock it. It was his room and his alone. He didn't have anyone he had to share things with.

"Check this out," Zeke said, cramming an Oreo in his mouth. "Just . . . got it."

A model. A big one. He handed Boy the bag of Oreos and took the model off his desk and sat down on his bed. Boy sat next to him.

"The *Enterprise*," Zeke said. "Take me about a month . . . to do it right, anyway, paint and all."

It was the biggest model Boy had ever seen. It would probably be three feet long when it was finished. Zeke opened it up and fingered the zillion pieces. "Dad sent it to me. Cool, huh?"

"No joke."

To Boy, Zeke was *rich*. But he always shared his stuff. He was a military kid, moved around a lot, and he had all this army, navy, marines, even air force stuff—bombers and jets hanging from the ceiling, fully painted, all the decals; miniature battalions of army guys facing each other in a standoff on his dresser; four disarmed hand grenades and a steel army helmet; eight models of navy ships, nine with the *Enterprise*, and a model German tank; and a giant poster of John Wayne in the movie *The Sands of Iwo Jima* on the back of his door. He even had a blue blanket with *US Navy* in yellow on it. And a cafeteria-size mayonnaise jar full of pennies, nickels, and dimes.

But what Boy liked best were the bandoliers of spent machine-gun shells and the ammo boxes they came in, what they found at Bellows. Shiny golden brass. So *nice.*

Zeke jumped up. "Let's go."

Boy wanted to say, You go and I'll stay here and play with all your stuff.

They walked out, stopping to hang their heads under the kitchen sink faucet for a cool drink.

"Where you going, honey?" Zeke's mom said without turning away from the TV.

"Out."

"Ummm."

And that was that.

"Does she know you go to Bellows?"

"I've told her before."

"And she doesn't care?"

"She thinks Bellows Field is a ballpark."

"And you didn't tell her what it really is?"

Zeke humphed. "Why?"

Boy frowned. Some things about Zeke made him feel funny. And his mother, too. Not laugh funny, but kind of sad, almost.

Zeke didn't have a lot of friends, which Boy didn't understand. He was weird to his mother, but other than that he was a good guy. Boy frowned, thinking, Right—such a good guy I get him beat up because of me and Gabriel.

They headed toward the ridge, walking through the back-street neighborhoods with dirt-and-sand driveways and old boxy houses like Boy's.

Boy saw a black dog sleeping in the bushes by someone's house. Pilot suddenly came to mind.

Pilot?

Boy wrinkled his forehead, wondering where he'd gotten *that* dumb idea. A made-up dog? That saved his life? He shook his head. *He* was the strange one. Not Zeke and his mom.

12

BY THREE O'CLOCK they'd hiked to the top of Ka'iwa ridge, where they could look back down and see the entire town of Kailua. But Zeke kept going; what he wanted was on the far side.

Bellows Field was an old, half-abandoned army air force base, a mysterious and forbidden military reservation that slept in its private oasis by the sea. It was a restricted area and no civilian could go in there without a pass.

They crossed under the barbed-wire fence.

Boy had never gone beyond that point before. He prayed that Daddy would never find out about it.

Posted signs blared KAPU! KEEP OUT! But Boy and Zeke gazed over the glory of crumbling bunkers from World War II, long weedy bushes and dry trees with thorns on them, dusty roads and a blue, blue sea beyond, gleaming under the sun.

A sudden breeze rose up and rustled the

brush on the ridge. "I know where there's some deserted barracks," Zeke said. "Look. You can see the roof."

Dirt slipped away as they stumbled down the crumbly ridge into the dry brush and down into the thorny, dusty trees and down along the trails that crossed beneath them, trails made by soldiers who had long since pummeled the earth to powder. Here in the undergrowth were the treasures—olive-colored ammo boxes, lost helmets, abandoned canteens, and sometimes a knife or a shovel. But most of all, Zeke wanted the spent machine-gun shells and the clips that had once held them together. These he gathered up and clipped back into long bandoliers that he wore across his chest when he roamed the streets of his neighborhood.

They came to what used to be a road. It had once been paved, but now it was nothing but a dusty potholed truck path where Boy and Zeke crept, their eyes cocked like land mines.

Boy saw something move, back in the trees. He stopped and squinted. Nothing. He knew it was a dog. His excitement sapped right out of him.

"What?" Zeke whispered.

"I saw something move. In there."

"I don't see anything."

"Something was there."

"Probably a mongoose."

"It was bigger than a mongoose."

They crept on, like soldiers stalking the enemy. They came to a shack, its windows broken out or shot out.

The boards creaked when they climbed the two steps. The porch sagged and the door was gone. Inside, dust and silence.

When they stepped back out into the sunlight, they saw them. Four of them.

Zeke gasped and stepped back.

The dogs slunk through the trees like wolves. There were four of them. They looked like regular dogs but they didn't act like them, didn't move like them. No.

Boy froze and the dogs crept through the trees, looking up and stopping and going on, then stopping to look up again. Boy's eyes swelled. He could taste the fear, like the taste of rust on the dead car by the insane dog, like the snarl and stench of the pit bull slamming into the chain-link fence, the bowing-out fence that hit him, but now there was no fence, nothing but open space and dog eyes looking, and his knuckles went white where he gripped the doorway.

The dogs paced, watching them.

Zeke eased down off the porch and picked up a rock.

"What are you *doing*?" Boy whispered.

"I'm gonna throw this at them. They're scared of us. Watch." Zeke cocked his arm.

"Wait!" Boy said.

A single tear trailed from the corner of one of Boy's eyes. But he wasn't crying; inside, his heart thundered and he wanted to run, to climb a tree, even to throw rocks. But rocks would make them mad, and they'd attack. "Don't." His voice cracked.

Zeke stood ready, but didn't throw.

Two dogs came out of the trees, and Zeke raised the rock again.

"No!"

The rock bounced into the trees and the dogs ran off.

Then they came back.

"Grab some rocks!" Zeke said.

Boy couldn't move.

"Come on! Grab some!"

Boy forced himself off the porch. He grabbed as many rocks as he could cram into his pockets.

Zeke started back toward the road they had just come down. Boy followed. "Why'd you throw it? *Why?*"

"They were getting too close."

"They were just looking at us. Now they're mad."

They walked fast and the dogs shadowed

them, glimpsed in the trees, silhouettes, blurs. Whenever they got too close Zeke tossed another rock and they ran off.

But always they came back.

Boy and Zeke scrambled back up the ridge, throwing rocks at the dogs until they had none left and had to throw whatever they could find along the way.

The dogs followed.

They got close once, and growled. Boy yelled at them. The dogs paced faster, the sound exciting them.

"Ghaaahhh!" he yelled again.

The dogs sidled and loped and side-glanced, stopping now and again to listen and smell the fear lingering in the air.

Boy and Zeke lunged to the top of the ridge and bellied under the fence and stumbled down to where there were houses and cars and people.

And still the dogs followed them, right under the fence.

Loping. Smelling. Following.

Until they reached the first street.

Then they slunk back into the brush and vanished.

13

WHEN BOY WALKED into his yard, he heard shouting. He went around back and stood listening by the garbage cans. His father's voice filled the yard.

"That's it! I had it with that boy. He's *out* of here!"

"Wesley, wait . . . he's just a boy. He—"

"He ain't just a boy and don't you tell me that one more time."

"He's only *fourteen*. He just needs to feel independent. It's normal. Maybe if you spent more time with him, he—"

"How can I spend more time when he don't even come home? Tell me that, you so smart."

He slammed out of the house, slammed the truck door.

Boy peeked around the side of the house just as Daddy started the truck. The engine roared and dust rose in the driveway when he backed out. He screeched to a stop out on the road, then took off.

Except for a handful of chickens pecking roaches out of the dry grass, the place was dead still.

Boy opened the kitchen door.

Mama wasn't there, but he could hear Mike and Jason making truck and explosion sounds in their room.

Boy set his books on the kitchen table and went to the sink to wash his dusty face and hands. When he was done, he turned around and saw Mama lying on the couch in the living room, the crook of an arm over her eyes.

He dried his hands on his T-shirt and walked closer and stood looking at her. Her tired old T-shirt. Limp hair and bare feet. The plain gold band on her puffy wedding finger.

"Hi, Boy," Mama said with her arm still over her eyes.

"How'd you know it was me?"

"I always know when it's you. When I hear quiet sounds and no voice, then I know it's Boy. Come here. Sit down by me." She patted the couch, eyes still covered.

Boy sat and she took her arm off her eyes and touched his wrist. "I guess you heard Daddy."

"Yeah."

"He's mad at Damon."

"He's always mad at Damon."

Mama rubbed her eyes. "No, not always."

She was silent for almost a minute. Boy thought she might have gone back to sleep. He started to get up.

"There's something I haven't told you about Daddy, Boy."

Boy didn't like the sound of that.

Mama peeked up and saw his worried face. She smiled. "Daddy used to be just like Damon, Boy. Those two are chips off the same piece of wood. When Daddy was in the tenth and eleventh grades, he used to run around with a rough bunch of boys, all of them trying to be tough. Like Damon's friends.

"But inside, Daddy was so nice. Still, he hung around those boys who were always getting into trouble. But it was impossible for Daddy to do anything more than *act* tough. Because he wasn't a mean person. He didn't have it in him to talk stink to anybody.

"By twelfth grade he passed through that stage, thank heaven. Or else I wouldn't have married him."

Mama closed her eyes and went on. "But Damon has gone *beyond* what Daddy was. And it scares Daddy."

She opened her eyes and cupped a hand over Boy's cheek. "He loves you kids so much, Boy, so very much. Don't get him wrong when he yells at Damon. He does it because he loves him."

Her voice cracked, and she sat up and wiped a tear away with her thumb. "Daddy loves Damon, and that's why he gets mad, because he wants so much for him, and all Damon does is treat him like dirt."

Boy stared at Mama a moment, then said, "If he loves him . . . if he loves him, he shouldn't yell at him."

Mama sighed. "One thing Daddy feels worse about is you."

"Me?"

"And I feel bad, too. You are so sweet and so good that you get lost, because . . . well, because we don't have to worry about you like we do Damon and Venita." She pulled Boy's head over to her shoulder and hugged him. "Daddy and I love you so much. We don't say that enough, do we?"

Boy pulled himself free. "It's okay, Mama."

"Daddy's so worried about Damon that he doesn't know what to do. Have you seen him? Damon?"

"I saw him at school. After school. He was with Bobby and Joker and Rick."

"The famous Cudas." Mama frowned and pushed herself up. "Those boys are nothing but trouble."

"Mama, he's the *leader* of those guys."

Mama rubbed her hand over her face. She put her arm around Boy. "Come help me get your brothers in the bathtub."

They stood up.

"You know, I'm proud of you for taking over Damon's paper job."

Boy looked down.

"No, really," Mama said. "Me and Daddy are *very* proud. He told me how you are afraid of Mr. Cruz's dogs, but that you go in there anyway and do your job."

Boy couldn't look at Mama. He *didn't* go in there. He was too scared, just like he was scared of Gabriel and Crowboy. Just like he couldn't stand up for Zeke. Just like he was scared to make Damon stop butting in, and now Damon was on the edge of big trouble with Crowboy because of him.

"It's not Mr. Cruz's dogs that scare me," Boy said. "It's the other ones."

"What other ones?"

"The wild ones."

"Wild ones?"

Now he looked at her. "The jungle dogs. You know, the ones Rick always talks about."

"I thought that was just a rumor, like Bigfoot."

"No, Mama. Those dogs are for real. I seen them."

"You *have*?"

Boy hesitated, then said, "Not only me, other guys, too."

Mama shook her head. "Such imaginations. Come on, let's throw those little rats in the tub."

Later that evening, while Mike and Jason were trying to go to sleep, and Venita had long been on the telephone with Slime, and Daddy had come back and checked out on the couch with a beer, Boy took his essay and a clean sheet of paper and sat out on the porch.

Zorro came slinking out of the bushes and jumped up next to him. Boy reached over and scratched his ears and Zorro arched his back. "You like that, huh?" Zorro started purring, but then jumped off the porch and crouched in the dusty yard, his tail twitching.

The light wasn't so good on the porch, so Boy moved out into the yard and sat cross-legged where he could see by the glow of the streetlight.

He read his essay, then looked out across the street, chewing on his pencil.

Finally, he turned the essay over, and on the clean sheet of paper, started to write.

I look up to my dog because he saved my life.

His name is Pilot, and if it wasn't for him I'd be dead.

One day I took him over the ridge and down into Bellows Field. It was a hot day. The back of my neck was roasting. We hiked in the dust to the top of Ka'iwa ridge and looked down on Bellows. I was afraid to go down in there. It was too quiet. But I wanted to collect bullet shells so I could make a bandolier with them.

Pilot went down first. He slipped in the dry dirt.

When we got to the bottom, we started walking along an old road. We found a house that was empty and we went inside, but there was nothing in it but dust, so we came back out. And that's when we saw the wild dogs.

Pilot started growling.

The dogs came closer and closer and now they were growling, too. They didn't worry about Pilot because he was only one dog and they were four.

I grabbed him and pulled him into the house. But there were no doors to close so we ran out the back. The dogs saw us and chased us, not running fast, but fast enough.

I couldn't run as fast as they could. Pilot could, but he didn't. He stayed with me.

The dogs attacked us.

Pilot fought with all four of them and it sounded like the end of the world. But Pilot won, and the dogs limped off.

But Pilot was all cut and could hardly walk. His blood dripped out. It was warm and sticky and I had to carry him home. My arms and shirt were all red with Pilot's blood.

Me and my dad put him in his truck to take him to the vet, but before we got there, Pilot died.

I look up to Pilot, because he saved my life.

14

SOMETIME AFTER MIDNIGHT Boy woke up and heard the squeak of the screen door.

There was a shuffling sound, not footsteps, but a kind of quiet stumbling, and Boy popped up on one elbow. The door to his room flew open and a dark figure staggered over to the other bed and fell down on it.

"Damon?" Boy whispered.

"Shhh," Damon said, and then moaned. "Unnnh."

Boy threw off his covers. "What's wrong?"

"I said be quiet. . . . Ow! Ow! Ow! . . . Get a rag or something. . . . Get it wet and bring . . . bring it to me."

"What's wrong?"

"Shut up and get it."

Boy grabbed a T-shirt off the floor and ran into the bathroom. He soaked it in the sink, then squeezed it out and ran back. Damon was sitting on the edge of his bed, bent over with his arms folded into his stomach.

"What's wrong?"

"I'm cut."

Boy turned on the light.

"Shut that off!" Damon spit, and Boy obeyed, but not before he saw Damon's face, bruised and scratched and bloody and one eye swollen to a slit and a gash on his cheek with dried blood frozen down his neck.

"What *happened?*" Boy said.

"Gimme that."

Boy crouched down and held the wet shirt out to Damon, but Damon wouldn't take his hands away from his stomach.

He lay back, slowly. "You do it," he said. "Get . . . get the flashlight."

Boy got Damon's army surplus flashlight and turned it on. The yellow light was vague and flickering.

Boy lifted Damon's bloodied arms away. There was a dark, wet blotch on his shirt the size of a squashed tomato. He lifted the T-shirt. The cut was only about two inches long, but the meaty part just under the skin boiled out.

"Who did this?" Boy asked.

Damon groaned softly.

Boy whispered, "Crowboy."

"He going die," Damon said. "Ow! Ow! . . ."

Boy dabbed the wet T-shirt on the cut and Damon winced and grabbed Boy's arm and squeezed it. But he did not cry out.

"I need Daddy," Boy said. "You need a doctor."

"No! Don't—"

The light came on. Boy jumped. Damon closed his eyes and moaned.

Daddy stood in the doorway, taking it all in, and when he saw that there was blood, he hurried over and gently pushed Boy aside. He looked at the cut and studied Damon's beat-up face and put his hand on Damon's forehead.

A trail of blood leaked out of the cut. Daddy took the wet shirt from Boy and pressed it over the wound and said to Boy, "Hold this here until I get back." He went out.

Boy held the T-shirt on the wound, keeping pressure on it. Damon was silent. Every few seconds Boy looked over his shoulder at the door.

Daddy came back dressed and carrying a blanket. "Get your clothes on," he said to Boy.

At three-thirty in the morning, after two hours at the hospital, Daddy drove Boy home, then went back. The cut had not been as bad as it looked, but it was bad enough for eight stitches and a tetanus shot. Damon was in more danger of damage to the sight in one of his eyes than he was from the cut.

Boy tried to sleep but he couldn't. He'd have to get up soon anyway.

The phone rang.

Boy heard Mama mumbling. He lay there listening, and feeling Damon's blood on his hands, even though he'd scrubbed every last trace away.

At four o'clock he got up and got dressed and went out to sit on the porch to wait for the papers to be dropped off. When they came, he folded them and stuffed them into his bike bag. He walked his bike out to the street and headed off.

At the Cruz place he started down the dark road. He stopped and leaned into the darkness, then moved forward an inch. He stopped and reached for a paper. Once more he started down the road into the jungle.

He could feel a rubbery limpness growing in his legs, and a trembling. *I can do it. I am not afraid. I am not a coward.*

He made it to the dead place where he couldn't see anything but deep black shadows. Faster, he thought, just race, just punch through. *Go.*

A dog barked.

Then another, louder, louder, coming closer, racing toward him.

He threw the paper as far as he could into the darkness where the dogs were, and turned and pedaled for his life. A bat *whoof*ed past his cheek as he raced away.

15

BOY WALKED INTO CLASS only five minutes late and slunk over to his seat and sat staring at the back of Rose's head.

Behind him someone whispered, "*Arf, arf,*" followed by a stifled laugh. Boy glared toward the front of the room.

A piece of folded paper grazed his cheek and fell on his desk. He ignored it. But then he covered it with his hand.

"Before we get started today," Ms. Ching said, "let's see how some of you are progressing with your essays."

Desks and chairs screeched and shuffled. Three-ring binders popped open loudly. Four hands went up.

"Tiffany," Ms. Ching said.

Tiffany carefully lifted a sheet of paper out of her binder and clicked the binder shut.

"I look up to my mom because she can dance hula.

Hula used to be danced to honor the gods and chiefs. It was also danced to accompany poetry. When the missionaries arrived in the islands, they did not like hula because it offended them. They tried to abolish it. But the wisdom of Hawaii's royalty kept it alive. I look up to my mom because she is doing her part to preserve my heritage and keep hula alive."

Ms. Ching smiled and said, "That's very nice, Tiffany. So nice, in fact, that on your next revision if you'd just put a little more of your mother in there, I think you'll have it."

Tiffany sat back with her mouth open, holding the paper half raised in front of her.

Boy drew a cube and put Tiffany inside it. Under it he wrote, *Help me!* and grinned.

Then he frowned. The note that had landed on his desk was screaming, *Read me, read me!* But Boy knew it had to be from Gabriel. Boy drew a knife with fat drops of blood dripping off it, but then he thought of Damon's blood and quickly erased it.

Ms. Ching looked around the room. "Okay, who's next?"

Zero hands went up.

Boy took his glasses off and rubbed them with his shirt, seriously, hoping Ms. Ching would not call on him because he was busy.

"Hmmm," Ms. Ching said. "Martha, didn't I see your hand up earlier?"

"Yes, Ms. Ching."

"Well, let's hear what you have to say."

Martha started reading. She looked up to Susan B. Anthony because she had her own coin. As she read, Boy stared at the folded note. He slid it closer and picked it up and held it down by his stomach and opened it.

After school. Arf, arf.

Martha finished reading and Ms. Ching said her essay was very good and would she please rewrite it.

"Let's hear one more," Ms. Ching said.

Boy glanced around the room. Gabriel sat slumped in his seat, his legs going back and forth. Zeke sat slumped, too, like almost all the boys. But Marianne had her hands clasped on her desk, her hair perfect, her face perfect, her clothes perfect. Boy studied her until she felt his eyes on her and turned with a face that said, What are *you* looking at?

"Marianne," Miss Ching said, making Marianne jump. "Do you feel like sharing your work with us?"

Boy turned in his seat to watch her.

Marianne read, *"I look up to my dad's friend Nainoa Thompson because men like him are the future of these islands."*

Ms. Ching put her hand up and Marianne stopped.

"Pay attention, class. See how Marianne put a lot of thought into this opening. To say someone is the future of the islands is quite a sophisticated concept."

Marianne's face looked a little red.

"Please go on," Ms. Ching said.

"In 1980, Nainoa Thompson guided the double-hulled canoe Hokule'a *across the Pacific Ocean in search of Tahiti. He did this by dead reckoning, which means he did not use a sextant or a compass, which is how it was done by the Polynesian travelers hundreds of years ago. He used the stars and his intuition. After he reached Tahiti, he navigated the* Hokule'a *back to Hawaii.*

"I have heard Nainoa speak about these islands, about how crowded they are getting and how we need to return to the aina, the land. We have forgotten what it is to take care of ourselves.

"I look up to Nainoa Thompson because he helped me to see that if I don't stand up with other people like him and do something about preserving these fragile islands we live on, then one day there will be no Hawaii as we know it. There will only be useless land and junk heaps of rusted cars.

"Nainoa Thompson stands up for what is right and is not afraid of what anyone else says about him. I look up to him because he opened my eyes."

She stopped. The class was silent.

Ms. Ching looked at Marianne. "It is so satisfying to me to hear work like this."

Everyone turned to Marianne, who had her hands over her face peeking through the fingers.

Boy wrote *Somebody dies* where the bloody knife used to be.

Later, when the class was struggling on a page of math problems, Ms. Ching worked her way around the room reading everyone's essays. When she got to Boy, he gave her his, then looked back down at the math problems.

Ms. Ching read it and folded it and handed it back.

Boy took it. When she didn't walk away, he glanced up.

Ms. Ching hesitated, then smiled.

16

AFTER SCHOOL, Boy got lucky. He left quickly and escaped running into Gabriel.

When he got home, Damon was lying on the couch watching an old rerun of *Starsky and Hutch* on TV. A sash of bright white bandages circled his belly, with a lump of extra gauze over the cut. His damaged eye wasn't so puffy anymore, but it was dark red where white should have been. He glanced over at Boy, then looked back at the TV.

"Hey," Boy said. "How you feeling?"

Damon picked up the remote and turned the TV louder. You could probably hear it all the way out in the street.

Boy waited a moment, then started to walk away.

"He ain't heard the end of this, I tell you that."

Boy stopped. "What?"

Damon flicked his hand as if to say, Beat it.

In his room Boy sat on his bed and pulled out his essay. He read it again. What was it that had made Ms. Ching hesitate before she smiled at him? Or did he imagine that? And what about Gabriel's threat?

Boy lay back and put a hand under his head and watched a fly sweep the corners of the screened window, buzzing and stopping, buzzing and stopping, and after a while Boy closed his eyes and the paper slipped from his hand and the fly circled the room twice and flew out the door.

Daddy came home early, before Mama and Mike and Jason. When Boy heard the truck door slam, he went out to the kitchen to look for something to eat.

Daddy walked in and stopped to check on Damon on the couch. Boy grabbed a couple of Saloon Pilot crackers and leaned against the kitchen counter, looking over at his father and his older brother.

Then Venita burst in, fingering Slime's ring on the chain around her neck, smiling about something. But her smile vanished when she saw Daddy standing by the couch. Daddy said something, but Damon didn't answer him.

Venita stood by Daddy and said, "Damon! So stupid. So, so stupid." She went into her room, glancing once at Boy.

Damon turned the TV up another notch.

Daddy took the remote from him. He turned the TV off and called Boy over with a nod. He said, "Come, Damon. We going to see Gramma."

Damon blinked, so slightly you had to know him to see it. Like a lizard, Boy thought.

"Let's go," Daddy said. But Damon didn't move.

Boy worried that Daddy might explode. Usually he hardly said a word to anyone, a little bit here, a little bit there. But if you got him mad, watch out.

One time at dinner, when Damon was giving everybody smart mouth, Daddy pounded his fist on the kitchen table and everything on the table flew up, and when it all came back down, *man,* what a noise! Everybody shut up quick.

Boy shuddered when he remembered that.

Daddy stood over Damon with his hands on his hips and the muscles in his jaw working and his eyes slitting down. "Are you going to get up or do I have to make you?"

Damon, still not looking at Daddy, said, "You

can't make me do anything." Zorro jumped up into his lap.

"You don't want to find out what I can or can't do, son. Now, get up."

Damon started stroking Zorro, slowly, slowly.

"Now!" Daddy boomed.

Zorro leaped down and ran under the TV.

Damon slapped the couch and sat up. He winced, then stood.

In the truck, the whine of the engine was loud in the cab and the metal floorboard steamed under Boy's feet. He sat in the middle between two silent boulders. It was hot and his T-shirt stuck to his sweaty back. As always, the truck smelled of rotting grass.

It wasn't until they were almost to Gramma's house that Daddy spoke. "I saw old man Cruz today," he said. "He said his paper was way out by the street."

Boy didn't answer, but Daddy let it go.

They rode another mile in silence. Boy thought about Gramma Regis, who he didn't see that much anymore. But the memories of going up there were clear—the muddy trails in the jungle behind her house, the banana tree farms, the red dirt and sweet smells, and the bowl of mangoes and mountain apples that would be in her kitchen waiting for him and Damon. And the Rice Krispies Treats. Yeah! But now was different.

They only went to see her once a month, about. And Gramma was getting strange, too. Sometimes she didn't even remember who he was.

"How come we're going to Gramma's?" he asked.

"She needs our help."

"Is she sick or something?"

"No. Just getting old."

They turned off the highway and drove another half mile up a muddy sun-patched road crowded by a jungle of banana trees that stood motionless in the hot, humid inlands. The air was different here, thicker and smelling of rust. Boy breathed deeply, holding the sweetness in as long as he could, sunspots flickering in the cab.

Damon looked bored, staring straight ahead.

"Is Gramma dying?" Boy asked Daddy.

Daddy thought for a moment, then said, "Only her memory, son."

"Her memory?"

"And she's lonely."

When they got there, they parked on the short green thick-bladed grass and got out and walked up to the nicely painted old white house. Mango trees, more banana trees, red dirt, a jungle of ginger, and every bush and weed anyone could possibly ever think of came up and reached in and over the perfect lawn. A rock birdbath and plumeria tree stood just to the left of the front door. In the sky a bird passed and a small plane droned across the blue distance.

"Of all the places I maintain, I love this one the most," Daddy said.

"That's because you grew up here," Boy said.

"Yeah, but it's more than that. It's the land, yeah? This, right here, this is Hawaii."

"And the ocean," Boy added.

Daddy grinned. "And the ocean."

Daddy and Boy went up the steps and knocked.

Damon stayed at the truck, leaning against the front fender. Daddy looked back at him and frowned.

Daddy knocked again.

Damon was studying the mountains nearby, their steep flanks green and their tops softened by wispy clouds.

"Maybe she's not home," Boy said.

"She's home."

Almost five minutes passed before Gramma finally came to the door.

"Yes?" she said.

She looks so *small*, Boy thought. Even smaller than last time. Is she shrinking?

She wiped her hands on the red-and-white checkered apron around her waist, like she'd been washing dishes. Her hair looked like a thinning white ball on top of her head. But her eyes, huge in her big round glasses, were bright and clear. They just didn't recognize anyone.

"It's me, Mama. Wesley."

"Wesley?"

"Your son. Wesley."

"Oh. Wesley . . . you're Wesley?"

"I'm Wesley, Mama."

Boy followed Daddy in and Daddy said, "What's wrong? How come you called me?"

She looked puzzled and Daddy said, "You said someone was bothering you."

Gramma's eyes brightened. "Yes . . . oh yes. It was midgets."

"Midgets?"

"In the backyard. I saw them. Oh, they are so *noisy*. They keep me up all night. Who's this?" she said.

"Your grandson, Mama."

She forgot Boy and said to Daddy, "Young man, those midgets are trying to get inside the house, all the time trying to get in, all the time."

"Ahh," Daddy said. "That's not good." He scratched his chin and thought. "Wait right here, Mama."

Daddy tapped Boy's shoulder.

Boy followed him out to the truck. Daddy got out his leaf blower and a two-gallon fuel can. He poured some gas into the small tank, then strapped the blower on his back.

Damon was still looking at the mountains.

Daddy and Boy walked around the house to the backyard. Daddy grinned. "Let's go get 'um."

He started the blower, and together they walked all through the backyard, blowing at leaves and dirt and trees and puddles and weeds and anything else they could find to blow at, and all the while Gramma stood behind the screened back door watching.

"See any more midgets?" Daddy said, and Boy answered loud enough for Gramma to hear, "And don't you come *back,* you got that?"

Daddy grinned. He reached out and shook Boy's hand. "Good job, son. I think we got all of them."

Daddy's hand was rough and callused, fat from hard work. One punch from it would send you to China.

After they shook, Daddy scruffed Boy's hair gently.

They took the leaf blower back to the truck and went again to knock on the front door. This time Damon got up and came along with them. Daddy smiled at him, but Damon looked at his feet.

When Gramma opened the door, Daddy said,

"We chased every last one of those midgets away, Mama. They're not going to bother you anymore."

"Oh, you're so sweet, young man. How much do I owe you?"

"No charge." Daddy swept his arms around her.

"Oh." She pushed Daddy away. "Who are these nice young boys?"

"Damon and Boy, Mama. Remember? Your grandsons."

"My grandsons . . . Yes, yes. My grandsons," she said.

Boy gave her a hug.

Damon came up after him. "Hi, Gramma," he said. He gave her a long hug, like he really meant it. Daddy shook his head ever so slightly.

"You boys come back tomorrow and I will have some ice for you."

"Ice?" Damon said.

"Oh yes, ice. And strawberry syrup."

"Okay, Gramma," Damon said. "Sounds good."

They said goodbye, then got back in the truck and drove away. Boy glanced back at Gramma, holding back the door, looking as bewildered as a lost kitten.

As soon as they got out on the road, Daddy grinned and said, "If those midgets ever come back, she'll probably invite them in for tea, then call me to complain about how they drank up all her hot water.''

"How come she's like that?" Boy said.

"She's just old, son."

Damon said nothing, but he didn't look mad anymore. About halfway home he said, "Doesn't it scare you?"

"What?" Daddy said, surprised that Damon had spoken.

"Gramma. Doesn't it scare you how she is?"

Daddy thought for a moment. "No, son. It just makes me sad."

"I like to remember when she wasn't like that," Damon said.

"Me too, Damon," Daddy said. "Me too."

"It's weird."

"It's life."

17

AT FOUR O'CLOCK the next morning Boy got up to deliver papers. He sat scratching his chest on the edge of his bed. Across the room Damon rolled over. Boy stood and dressed in the dark. When he reached the door, Damon coughed, then said, "Wait. . . . I'm coming with you."

"You don't have to. I can do it."

"Okay, fine. I'm coming anyway."

Boy crept through the house to the porch and went out to get the papers, which had already been dropped off. He brought them back to the porch and untied them and started folding and pounding and stacking them. Boy wanted to tell Damon to back off, he could do it himself. But he was scared he might make Damon mad.

A few minutes later Damon limped out. He eased down next to Boy, holding a hand over his stomach. The one eye was still bloodred in the white part and the other was edged with a dark bruise. "Gimme some papers," he said, and Boy handed him a stack.

Out under the dim streetlight a cat scurried across the street and vanished under a car. In the distance the ocean whispered, a quiet rushing sound that never ceased, and in the beach parking lot across the street a single light made the whole world seem lonely. Boy liked it, though, the early morning. And even though he didn't like the way Damon kept watching over him, he didn't mind having him there now, folding papers. It was like back in the good days.

When they were done, Boy stuffed the papers into his bike bag. He cleaned his glasses with his shirt, put them on, and he and Damon rode off into the cool darkness.

Damon watched Boy deliver papers and only once had something to say to him. "This guy at this house," he said. "He don't find his paper in his driveway, then he going get mad. Trust me, punk. You don't want to get no complaints."

So Boy made sure the paper got on the driveway.

"Sometimes when I felt like it, I tossed it under his car," Damon added. "Still on the driveway, yeah?"

When they got to the Cruz place, they stopped and sat on their bikes at the road that went into the trees.

Damon grinned and his beat-up face looked hideous in the darkness. "Go," he said.

Boy inched ahead, his bike wobbling because he was going so slow. There was a rustling in the bushes on one side and he rode all the way over on the other side.

He stopped at the spot where he could see neither Damon nor the Cruz place. The rustling noise went on a second longer. Then it, too, stopped.

Boy grabbed a paper and threw it as far down the road as he could, then turned and wheeled out of there, pumping, pumping, gaining speed, flying almost, and the rustling came back, and the growling. He zipped out past Damon to the street and down toward the next neighborhood.

Damon rode after him, laughing his head off.

After the papers had been delivered, Boy stopped again at the viewpoint to watch the sky lighten and to look out over the sea.

Damon kept going, then circled back. He sat on his bike. "How come you always stop here? It's weird."

"Why is it weird?"

"Something about you is off."

Boy looked out toward the sea.

Damon sat back on his bike and pulled the front wheel up, doing a wheelie. He held it up a moment, then let it plop back down. His bruised face glowed in the sunrise, the sky clean of clouds and the mountains inland waking green in the light. Below them the ocean rolled on and on in its whispery hush, as it had from its beginning and would till its end.

Damon lifted his shirt to check his wound. Boy winced, and thought, Those stitches are my fault. It was my problem that started it, mine and Gabriel's. It was just that Damon had to butt in. Boy squeezed the handgrips, then let go.

"How do they feel, the stitches?"

Damon dropped his shirt. "Still hurts. Crowboy going pay."

"Forget Crowboy. You'll get hurt even worse! Maybe you'll get other people hurt, too. Gabriel is *my* problem, not yours."

"Fine. He still going pay."

"No!"

"Check out that old fut down there. Bringing out his canoe."

Boy turned to see Buzzy dragging his canoe down to the water.

"That's your friend, yeah?" Damon said.

"How do you know he's my friend?"

"I got spies."

"Pshhh."

Damon waved him off. "I going home. You're too weird for me."

18

DAMON RODE OFF.

Boy hid his bike in the bushes and climbed down the slope, careful not to step on Gilbert again. But Gilbert wasn't there today.

Buzzy saw Boy and waved. He pushed his canoe into the ocean and stood knee-deep beside it. "Got an extra paddle," he said.

Boy slogged into the water, and climbed in. Buzzy pushed the canoe farther out and slipped aboard himself. "What a day," he said.

They paddled to the flat island and then around it and on down toward the marine base. The ocean was flat and peaceful and so silky that neither of them spoke for the first twenty minutes.

Finally, Boy said, "You ever see any sharks out here?"

"Couple. By the island."

"Aren't you scared of them?"

Buzzy laughed. "Sharks? Naah. They don't bother me. They just looking for something to eat. If I was swimming, I would keep my eyes open. Still, I wouldn't be scared of them."

A few minutes later Boy said, "Why?"

"Why what?"

"Why wouldn't you be scared of sharks? What if they want to eat *you*?"

"Well . . ."

Buzzy thought and paddled and Boy paddled in the same rhythm. The canoe slipped ahead in smooth thrusts, the turquoise sandy bottom gliding by below.

Finally, Buzzy stopped paddling. He half turned in his seat. "Okay," he said. "This is why I'm not scared of them. People don't like things because why? Because they don't understand it, yeah? When you are a small kid, you are afraid to go in the ocean because you don't know how to swim. Then when you learn, you go ocean every day, no problem."

Boy said, "I guess."

Buzzy thought another moment. "Okay. When you in school and some kid tells you he going broke your head after school, you are afraid. Then maybe you fight with him and you see that he was just a loudmouth and pretty soon you not afraid of him. Right?

"And so," Buzzy went on, "with a shark it's

the same thing. First you are afraid because you heard about some kid who lost a leg, or you heard about that lady on Maui who was swimming and got attacked. Sure that happens, and sure you got to think about it. But when you know sharks, you ain't scared. You just learn to live with them. Still, you got to be smart. Take precautions. But if they eat you, they eat you. Your time is up, yeah?"

Boy stopped paddling. "Well, are you afraid of *anything*?"

Buzzy snickered. "Sure. Plenty things."

"Like what?"

"Like . . . okay, like dying. Like what going happen to me when I check out. I wonder if there's going be nothing, or if there's going be some place where everybody look like ghosts, or if everybody going be all dressed up in white, or if I going come back again and be a spider or a cat or what, I don't know. Nobody knows. Plenty people think they do. But they don't. In my opinion."

Buzzy smiled to himself and added, "I haven't said that much to anyone in a long time."

Boy started paddling, harder, putting his whole body into it. Stroke, pull, stroke, pull. Buzzy turned around. "What you doing back there?"

"Paddling."

"How come so hard? You late for school?"

"No."

"Then what?"

"I don't want you to die."

Buzzy laughed. "*Die?* From what?"

"Working too hard."

"Working hard is what's keeping me *alive,* boy. That's why I come out and paddle. Every day I do this. Use it or lose it. You never heard that?"

"No."

"True. Use it or lose it. Hah!"

Boy stopped paddling and Buzzy turned around again. "Now what?"

"I'm letting you work. So you can use it."

"Sheese!" Buzzy said.

19

DAMON WENT TO SCHOOL with his face looking like a car wreck. Daddy gave him and Boy a ride.

They sat three in a row in the front seat. When Boy's arm rubbed up against Damon's, Damon leaned closer to the door. No one said a word the whole way.

When Damon got out at the high school, he didn't thank Daddy for the ride or close the door. He didn't even look back.

Daddy shook his head and watched him walk away. Boy pulled the door shut and Daddy drove on to Boy's school.

"See if you can find Damon after school and walk home with him," Daddy said. "I know what he's thinking, and what he's thinking is trouble."

"I will," Boy said, and Daddy drove off.

Boy stood there watching him go, trying to remember. What was it that made Damon change from a nice brother into a tough guy?

But Boy couldn't think of any one thing. It must have been something that happened slowly.

There was one time, though, Boy remembered. Back when he was about ten, and Damon was twelve. Daddy used to take Damon down by Makapu'u to go shore casting. Week after week after week, just the two of them. Sometimes Boy went, too, and Damon was always watching out for him, like helping him get his hook unstuck from the rocks, or taking a fish off the line because Boy didn't like to see that big fish eye looking up at him with the gills pumping. But Damon never seemed to mind helping him.

But anyway, one weekend Damon went camping with a friend down the coast at Malaekahana. And on that same weekend, Daddy got an urge to go shore casting. So he asked Boy to go. And since Damon wasn't there, Boy spent a lot of time talking with Daddy. Boy liked it. And Daddy seemed to like it, too.

Then, when they came home, and Damon came home from camping, Boy and Daddy talked about their fishing trip at the dinner table. And as Damon listened, his eyes narrowed, and he wouldn't look at either of them, just at his plate.

That night, Damon went to sleep early, with his face to the wall. He hadn't said one word to Boy, or to Daddy. And maybe something might have started to change in Damon then. After that,

Damon started coming up with reasons *not* to go fishing with Daddy.

Just because Boy and Daddy had a good time fishing without him?

Right after school Boy walked over to the high school and sat around on the grass watching for Damon like Daddy said. He leaned back on his elbows, then sat up and fingered the grassy indentations in his skin.

An hour passed, but Damon never showed up.

Finally, Boy saw Joker coming out and asked him where Damon was.

"Who knows?" Joker said. "He left early, him and Bobby and Rick."

"Early?" Boy said.

"Like at lunchtime. I would be with them now except I had detention, stupid Mr. Boyle."

"Where'd they go?"

"Why I should tell you?"

"I was supposed to walk home with him."

"Gotta be kidding." Joker laughed and walked away.

Boy looked around. Maybe he could find Venita. She might know where Damon was.

The only place he knew to look was the car

wash where Slime worked. Funny, he thought, how she'd been going out with Slime for about three months now and still Boy had never even seen him. In Boy's mind Slime was about six feet tall with oily service station clothes and black hair, maybe shaved around the ears and long on top. And he had to be greasy to get the name Slime. Did he know Damon had come up with that name? Venita was so mad the first time Damon called him Slime that she'd scratched his arm. But Damon just laughed. Venita cried and Damon loved it when she got all bent like that. Boy had to admit that the name was funny. Slime. Shee.

The first thing he saw at the car wash was flashing blue lights. Cop car. And a red-and-white Fire Department rescue truck.

A crowd of people stood around staring at somebody on the ground. Gilbert, the guy from the beach, was there, too, pacing back and forth like he couldn't stand still.

Boy squeezed through the crowd. Some woman, lying on the dirty pavement with her eyes closed and an oxygen mask over her mouth and nose. Can't be dead, Boy thought. If she was dead, they'd cover her face with a blanket and take that mask off, like on TV. Even so, the sight of her lying there like that made Boy feel kind of sick.

Nobody said a word except for the two rescue guys who were crouching around her, talking in almost a whisper.

Boy backed out of the crowd. Gilbert was looking in a trash can now.

Boy frowned, and looked around and found a kid with *Kailua Wash & Wax* on his shirt. "What happened?" Boy asked.

"Passed out while she was going through the car wash."

Boy shuddered. "Spooky."

"No joke."

"Is Sli . . . uh, is Herbie here?"

The boy looked around. "There, over by the 7-Eleven."

Boy turned to look where the kid was pointing, but all he could see was a woman with a man and a small girl on the man's shoulders. They were walking the other way, slowly.

"Where?" Boy asked.

"There. The guy with the kid."

"That's Herbie?"

"That's him."

Boy squinted. "Hey . . ." he said. That was *Venita* with him. Jeese, fake me out, Boy thought. From behind she looked like that little kid's *mother*.

The car wash guy said, "The kid belongs to the

lady who passed out. Was in the car with her. He's trying to cheer her up. So she won't get bad dreams, yeah?"

Boy walked over toward Venita, whose arm was around Herbie's waist, her thumb hooked through one of his belt loops. With that little girl they looked like . . . *married.*

"Venita," Boy called, and she turned.

"Boy!" she said, her eyes bright. "What are you doing here?"

"I'm . . . I'm looking for Damon. Daddy said I was supposed to walk home with him."

"Why?"

Boy shrugged and looked at Slime, to check him out.

Venita said, "Herbie, this is my brother James. But we call him Boy."

Herbie wasn't anything like the Slime guy in Boy's head. He was shorter than six feet, and he didn't have dirty black hair and zits. He had brown hair and looked Japanese-haole-Hawaiian, or something. He looked like a movie star, almost. His blue *Kailua Wash & Wax* work shirt was spotless. He stuck out a hand, holding on to the girl's knee with his other hand. "Boy," he whispered, so softly you could hardly hear it. "Nice to meet you."

Boy said, "Hi," and the two of them shook.

Slime smiled and looked into Boy's eyes for a second, then turned to Venita.

Venita had a look Boy had never seen before, soft and dreamy. Slime looked that way, too, only shy, like he might jump if somebody sneezed.

"So have you seen Damon?" Boy said to Venita.

"No."

"Hey!" Slime suddenly called, looking over to where Gilbert was digging through the trash can. Gilbert looked up. Slime held out a five-dollar bill, folded once between his fingers. Gilbert hurried over and grabbed it, then left, saying nothing.

Boy looked at Slime a moment. Then he raised his chin. "See you around . . . Herbie," he said.

Herbie dipped his head at Boy, and Venita hooked her arm through his elbow, and the little girl studied Boy.

Damon was way off about this guy.

Boy went home alone.

20

THAT NIGHT about eight o'clock someone knocked at the front door. Daddy and the twins and Boy were watching a *Magnum, PI* rerun, the one where the Lads trap Magnum in his house.

Boy turned when he heard the knock and saw Ms. Ching standing on the porch, fuzzy through the screen.

Daddy got up and ran his fingers through his hair, then opened the door.

"Come, come," he said, waving Ms. Ching inside.

Boy stood and wiped his hands on his shorts and gaped, but the twins didn't even turn away from the TV.

Mama, who was reading the paper at the kitchen table, got up and walked over.

"I'm sorry for coming so late," Ms. Ching said. "We had a meeting at school." Had Ms. Ching called earlier? Why was she here?

"You're welcome anytime," Mama said, and motioned for Ms. Ching to sit at the kitchen table. Mama took the paper to the counter, then got three glasses and filled them with the lemonade she had just made that evening.

Daddy turned the TV down and came and sat across from Ms. Ching, with his arms crossed over his chest.

Boy stood behind him, watching.

"Well," Ms. Ching said, then paused. She put her hand on the table and looked at it. Then she looked up. "Boy seems to have a talent for writing, and . . . well, I think he could be doing far better in school than he is. I thought we might make a team and push him a little."

Daddy raised his eyebrows. He and Mama looked at Boy, then at each other. A world seemed to pass in that look.

"I had the class write an essay on someone they looked up to in their lives. Boy's was . . . different. It moved me. He wrote about Pilot."

Daddy and Mama waited for more.

"Pilot," Ms. Ching said. "Your dog . . . that saved Boy's life."

"Saved his *life*?" Daddy said, putting both hands on the table.

Mama touched Ms. Ching's wrist and said, "We don't have a dog."

"Oh, that's right. He died, didn't he?"

Daddy said, "We don't have a dog and we never had a dog and we probably won't ever get a dog. Hard enough to feed just us."

Boy looked at the floor.

Ms. Ching said, "Boy?"

When he didn't answer, she said, "Why don't you show your parents your essay?"

Boy frowned and went to his room, never lifting his gaze from the floor. When he came back, he handed the paper to Ms. Ching. She handed it to Daddy. He and Mama read it.

"He never had a dog," Daddy said. "He's afraid of them. And he knows better than to go into Bellows Field, I tell you that."

Mama put the essay on the table and stared at it.

"I . . . I don't know what to say," Ms. Ching said.

There was a silence, except for Magnum, who was still trying to talk his way past the Lads.

Daddy said to Boy, "How come you wrote this?"

Boy shrugged.

"Boy," Ms. Ching said, and Boy peeked up.

She stopped to think. Then, "Listen," she said. "I have an idea. Let's turn this into a story, okay? It's so good. I know you can write more, and to tell you the truth, I'd really like to *read* more. Can you do that?"

Boy nodded. What more was there? Maybe Pilot could live. Maybe he could . . .

"Do you think you can also write another essay on someone you look up to? One that's . . . one with a real person in it?"

"Yeah. I guess."

"Good."

Ms. Ching pushed her chair back and said to Mama, "What's important to me is how Boy thinks and how he can express himself on paper." She stood up.

Daddy stood, too, not looking at Boy.

Ms. Ching put her hand on Boy's shoulder. "I really do love what you wrote." She tapped his arm twice and said, "See you in school."

After she left, Daddy looked at Boy and said, "A dog? Why a dog?"

Boy shrugged.

"It was good, though," Mama said, but Boy didn't look at either of them.

Daddy puffed up his cheeks, then said, "Go get your pencil and a new paper and sit here and get to work. This time, you write about a real person or a real dog."

Boy started to leave, but stopped when Daddy said, "How come? You don't even like dogs."

"It just came to me, that's all."

Daddy raised his eyebrows. "Just do your best, son."

* * *

When Venita came home, Boy was in bed. But he couldn't sleep. He was still thinking about how weird it was having his teacher in his house.

The door to his room opened and light from the hall spilled in. Boy squinted.

"You awake?" Venita asked.

"Yeah."

"Herbie said you were a nice kid."

Boy thought about getting mad about being called a kid. But he said, "I can't believe he gave that Gilbert guy five dollars."

"Why can't you believe it?"

"Well . . . I don't know. I just can't."

"Auntie Irma went out with him in high school, you know. Before he got messed up."

"Not! Gilbert?"

"It's true. Weird, yeah?"

"You're lying. How come I never heard that before?"

"Don't tell anyone I told you that, because I was supposed to keep it to myself."

"Why?

"Think about it, Einstein."

"Who told you?"

"Daddy."

Boy thought. That was so *weird*. Gilbert and

Mama's sister, Auntie Irma. He shook the idea away. "Well, anyway, Herbie's a pretty nice guy."

"Of course he's nice. You think I would go out with just any old dumb guy?"

"Well . . . ," he said. Until today, dumb guys were *all* he'd thought she'd gone out with. Slime guys, like Damon said.

Venita said, "He's kind of like Daddy, don't you think?"

"Herbie?"

"Yeah. Shy."

"Daddy's *shy*?"

"You live in a cardboard box or what? Of course. He's just not shy around here. You watch next time he takes you somewhere. Why do you think he always goes fishing? Because he doesn't have to talk to anybody, that's why."

Boy thought about that. Shy? Naah. Was he? "Well, anyway, Herbie's okay."

"See why I hate it when Damon calls him Slime?"

"Yeah."

"Well . . . oh, the lady is better. She was diabetic."

She closed the door softly.

Gilbert and Auntie Irma. Shee.

* * *

Damon came home about eleven. His voice and Daddy's were muffled sounds in the front room. Not angry, just two people talking.

When Damon came into the bedroom, he slammed on the light and Boy sat up. The bright light hurt his eyes. Damon took out his Discman and put the headset on. The drumbeat sent out irritating scratchy sounds.

"Where were you?" Boy said.

Damon lifted the headset off one ear. "What?"

"Where *were* you?"

Damon grinned. "None of your business."

Boy studied him. "Why are you like this? You used to be nice. Now you're like Rick."

"And what's that like?"

"Dress in black, hang around troublemakers, stay out all night, talk bad to Daddy, always got a chip on your shoulder. And that Cuda thing you say, fight or die, fight or die. Like Rick. Is that what you want? To fight? Look at your face."

Damon dipped his head to the rhythm. "Way it is, little man." He grinned and lay back on his bed with the headset blasting so loud you could dance to it. If you felt like dancing. Which Boy didn't.

Boy said, "How come you always give Daddy a hard time?"

Damon lifted the headset off again. "What?"

"How come you always gotta fight with Daddy?"

"Who's fighting?"

"You are. All the time arguing, him saying, Do this, do that, and you saying, Forget it, I do what I want."

"He can't tell me how to live my life. And you don't know what end of your body your head's at," Damon said. "Get out of my face." He put the headset back on.

Boy got up and turned off the light.

Damon chuckled in the dark.

Boy lay back on his bed and covered his head with his pillow. He didn't like the sound of that chuckle. There was something ugly in it, something bad.

21

AT NINE O'CLOCK on Saturday morning Boy was out in the yard washing Daddy's truck, a chore he did every weekend. Venita had taken the twins to the beach, and Damon was still sleeping. He could sleep until two or three in the afternoon if you let him. But Damon had chores, too, like the garbage.

Daddy was sitting on the porch with his feet on the steps and a pan of gasoline between them. Mama sat next to him, her arm across his shoulder, watching him clean the parts to his lawn mower.

After Boy finished washing the truck, Daddy said, "Go wake up Damon. Auntie Irma's coming over."

Mama smiled and squeezed Boy's leg as he slipped past and went into the house.

Boy stood over Damon, who was asleep on his stomach, his Discman on the floor. He shuddered when he remembered the chuckling sounds. What bad thing was in Damon's head?

"Hey," Boy said, nudging his shoulder. "Get up. Daddy said." Trying to wake up Damon was like trying to wake up a bag of rice. Boy nudged him again, harder. "Damon."

When Damon still didn't move, Boy went into the kitchen and got an ice cube. He ran it along Damon's back.

"*Ahhhh!*" Damon said, whipping around. He grabbed Boy's wrist and took the ice away. "You want to *die*?"

"Daddy says get up. Auntie's coming over."

"What am I, his slave?" Damon reached over for Boy's alarm clock and turned it toward him. "Ten-fif—Shhh." He lay back down and put his arm over his eyes. "Get out of here."

"You gotta get *up*. I ain't joking."

"Shut. Up."

Just then Daddy poked his head in the room. "Get up and get dressed. You want your auntie to think you're a lazybones?"

Damon didn't think that was funny. He took his arm off his eyes and sat up and threw the sheet away.

Boy was sitting on the steps next to Mama when Auntie Irma drove into the yard in a moving cloud of dust. She drove a little two-seat white Mercedes. Fifteen years old. But still, a Mercedes.

Boy winced when Auntie's dust cloud kept right on rolling over Daddy's freshly washed truck. He'd have to wash it again.

Mama stood up and waved.

Auntie Irma got out carrying a big paper bag with handles on it. "Hoo, so hot today," she said. She kissed Mama on the cheek, and said, "How's your tired old bones, Wesley?" and Daddy said, "Lucky for me they're a lot younger than yours," and Auntie said, "When I die, you going miss me and be sorry you were so mean to me."

Daddy grinned.

"Where's my boys?" Auntie said, meaning the twins, who she loved like crazy.

Mama said, "They're at the beach with Venita. They'll be back soon."

"What's in that bag?" Daddy said.

"Anniversary present from you to your in-laws, Wesley. Remember them? Fifty years next Friday. Here, sign this card. Both of you."

Daddy held up his gas-coated hands. "Emily can sign for me."

Mama took the card. "Let's see the bracelet, Sissy."

Auntie Irma looked into the bag and pulled out a small box. She opened it and showed it to Mama, and Mama said, "Ooh, very, *very* nice."

Auntie showed it to Boy, a shiny gold Hawaiian-style bracelet with black enamel lettering on it that spelled Gramma Makuakane's Hawaiian name, Kaho'opomaika'i, which means "she who brings blessings." She could show it off in Las Vegas.

Boy gave it back, thinking, *Auntie Irma and Gilbert.* Maybe he'd ask her about him, someday.

Daddy said, "So what you got for Grampa? A slot machine?"

Auntie slapped his arm, then reached in and pulled out a box. Daddy laughed. "You got your mama an expensive gold bracelet and you got Grampa a *rice maker?*"

"That's what he wants."

"Boy," Daddy said. "Go see what Damon's doing. Tell him to come out and see Auntie."

Damon was in the kitchen with his head in the refrigerator.

"Daddy said come outside," Boy said. Then, "There's some doughnuts in that bag on top." Daddy and Boy had gotten them after Boy finished delivering papers.

Damon stuffed a doughnut in his mouth. They went outside.

"Yahhh!" Auntie said, putting a hand to her face. "What happened to *you?*"

Damon chewed on the doughnut, touching

his eye. It was still red, but not so swollen. "Nothing," he said.

"Nothing, huh?" Auntie said. Then to Daddy, "What happened?"

"He got in a fight."

"How's the other guy look?"

That got a grin out of Damon.

Two little voices yelled, "Auntie!"

Across the street Mike and Jason broke away from Venita's grip and raced into the road. Mama gasped. Luckily there were no cars.

They ran into Auntie's open arms and she swept them both up, Mike saying, "What did you bring us?"

Mama said, "Hush, Mike. That's no way to greet Auntie."

"Come," Auntie said. "I got something in my car."

Damon went back inside the house.

"Damon," Daddy called, looking back over his shoulder. "Come back out here."

Damon didn't.

"He's so rude," Venita said.

Daddy scowled at the brownish motor parts lying in his gas pan. Then he stood, wiping his hands on a rag.

"Wesley," Mama said, putting a hand on his leg. "Not now, okay? Not while Sissy is here."

Boy said, "I'll go get him."

"No," Daddy said, sitting back down. "Mama's right. Leave him alone, if that's how he wants it."

Auntie came back with Mike and Jason and a plastic sack full of shiny red mountain apples. She gave one to each of them, then one to Boy.

"Where's the boxer?" she asked.

"He went inside." Boxer, he thought. Hmmph.

He remembered that time when Daddy took him fishing instead of Damon, that time Damon went camping. It wasn't long after that that he and Damon had gotten into their only fight. It made Boy sick to even think about it.

Boy shuddered, not because Damon had beaten him up, but because Damon had been so *angry*. Except for that insane dog that wanted to kill him, it was the worst memory Boy had.

For days after that fishing trip, Damon acted really weird, and nobody knew why. Mama tried to find out what was bothering him, but he just shrugged her off, saying, "Leave me alone."

Then one night in his room, Boy was drawing a picture of a shark in his journal. When Damon came in and saw it, he said, "What are you drawing a stupid fish for? You scared of fish. You can't even take one off the hook."

Damon had never talked to him like that before. Boy's mouth dropped open to say something back, but nothing came out.

"It's not only stupid, it's *ugly*. You can't draw a fish to save your life."

"It's not a fish! It's a shark and it's not ugly! Get away from me."

"What?" Damon said. He shoved Boy's shoulder, leaving an ugly pencil line that ran off the page.

Damon knocked his shoulder again, and again.

Boy threw himself into Damon. His journal fell open on the floor. Damon shoved him again, and knocked him down. When Boy stood up, Damon grabbed his shirt and slammed him up against the wall. He was stronger than Boy, way stronger, and Boy couldn't get away.

"If I say it's stupid and ugly, it's stupid and ugly, and not only that, you can't draw, you can't fish, you're a coward, and you're *nothing*! I don't ever want to see you drawing a fish again. It makes me sick to look at it. Everything about you makes me *sick*!"

Boy tried to push back.

Damon slapped his face.

"*Hey*!" Daddy yelled. "What's going on in here?"

Damon jumped back. Boy slumped to the floor.

His eyes had filled with tears as he tried to look at Daddy, everything wet and blurry.

Daddy put his hand around the back of Damon's neck and squeezed until Damon cried, "Stop it!"

"I catch you beating up on him again, you're going to be sorry, Damon, real sorry." He shoved Damon down on his bed and left, slamming the door behind him.

Damon leaped up and mashed the journal with his foot, then kicked it under Boy's bed. Then he went out of the room and out of the house and didn't come back till after midnight.

From then on, Boy had always watched his words around Damon.

Boy shook the memory away.

Daddy was looking at him, and Boy almost felt that Daddy knew what he was thinking. But Daddy looked down again and picked up another part in the gas pan. He scrubbed it with a toothbrush.

Mama got up and went inside with Auntie Irma, the twins, and Venita.

Boy washed Daddy's truck one more time, trying to get that fight out of his head.

22

SUNDAY WAS HOT, bright, and windless.

The screen door squeaked when Boy walked out of his house carrying a white plastic bucket and two bamboo fishing poles. He squinted into the sun, then stepped off the porch and headed toward the street.

The door flew open again and Damon came out. The swelling in his damaged eye had settled, but not the blur that made him blink like he'd caught a speck of dust under his lid. He, too, studied the sky, his hand under his T-shirt fingering the cut on his stomach, now covered by a small white bandage. He started to follow Boy, but stopped to fix his hair in the side mirror of Daddy's truck. When his hair was just right, they started down the street toward the canal.

"That paper job," Damon said.

"What about it?"

"Was good, you know? I miss it. You getting Mr. Cruz his paper yet?"

"I get it close enough."

"Right."

They walked in the dusty spillage along the side of the road while a stream of beach-going cars crawled by.

He could hear Damon breathing behind him, walking close. Boy frowned. Was there some reason Damon wanted to go fishing with him?

When they got to the bridge that crossed the canal, they turned toward the mountains. They walked behind a row of cars parked along the water until they found a spot where they could sit and fish for aholehole.

Boy gave Damon one of the bamboo fishing poles and each of them put a small piece of raw bacon on his hook, then split up and sat apart from each other, staring into the water.

Boy daydreamed awhile, then glanced over at Damon and almost gasped, because for a second, he thought Damon was *Daddy*—they looked so much alike, the way they fished so silently, so seriously. Boy had never noticed that before.

Damon looked back at Boy, probably feeling himself being stared at. Boy turned away.

Then he looked back. "Remember how Bobby hypnotized that chicken?"

"What about it?"

"Maybe we could try it with Zorro."

Damon grinned. "You gotta wake him up first. That might be hard."

They laughed. It felt so good, laughing with Damon.

But something they saw choked it off—Crowboy's truck, crossing the bridge. Crowboy and two other guys were in it. They drove slow, scanning the beach park with their eyes.

"Look," Boy said.

Damon didn't move.

"Look," Boy said again.

"I see 'um," Damon said, his eyes fixed on the water. Then he added, "I wonder how much those new tires cost."

"New tires?"

"His old ones went flat."

"What are you talking about?"

Damon lifted his hook to check the bait, then lowered it back down. *"Flat.* Man, I love that word. Flat like roadkill," he added.

"You did something to Crowboy's tires?"

"Ice pick," Damon said. "Look at my eye! I should have broke out his windows and cut up his seats, too!"

"Aw, man."

"He started it."

"No! *You* started it," Boy spit back. "You

138

started it by thinking you always have to *protect* me. *You* started it, not Crowboy. You think you're so tough, but you're just making trouble . . . for me, for you, for *everybody*. Why don't you just wise up?''

Silence.

Boy couldn't believe he'd said that.

Damon stared at Boy, his eyes slits.

Boy pulled up his bait and laid the pole on the ground and sat there with his knees up and his elbows crossed over them and his head down on his arms. He was so mad he was shaking. So what if Damon beat him up again?

"You better watch your mouth, little man," Damon said.

"That ain't no life, Damon, the Cudas, fight or die."

Damon spit into the water.

Crowboy's truck cruised by again, now with five guys in it, all of them looking, searching, and this time Boy knew who it was they were looking for.

23

THAT AFTERNOON Boy rode his bike to the jungle where Mr. Cruz lived. He started down the dirt road and stopped when he rounded the bend and could see neither street nor house. The sun was low and the dirt road in shadow.

He listened.

There were no rustlings in the trees or in the weeds. There was only the hum and grind of cars leaving the beach.

He walked his bike around the bend and when he came in view of the house, the Cruz dogs came charging out, barking. He turned his bike so that it stood between him and the dogs. His heart started thumping.

"Good dogs, good boys," he said, and as they whisked around him, he held out a hand, like Daddy had. Except his hand shook.

He pulled it back, then forced himself to stick it out again for them to sniff.

They pranced around the bike, circling him, growling low, and Boy, nearly crying, clicked his tongue. He spoke to them softly, and they quieted and came to nudge his trembling hand with wet noses.

Slowly, Boy put his bike down. He rubbed the two dogs around their ears. One lay down and rolled in the dirt with its paws up. Boy rubbed its belly with his foot and the dog's eyes closed to a lazy squint.

Boy felt a heaviness lift from him, something he did not even know was there until he felt it leave. He almost felt like laughing. He liked the scratchiness of the dog's fur and the looseness of its skin under his bare foot. Lazy old dog, nice lazy old dog.

No one came out of the house.

Boy surveyed the yard. It was sunny and quiet, so quiet Boy could hear flies buzzing. He leaned his bike against his leg and took off his glasses and absently cleaned them, not looking to see if they were even dirty. He squinted up at the sun. Nice day.

He turned his bike to leave and the Cruz dogs went with him, trotting ahead stiff-legged, leading him out to the road. They stopped and he rode past them, and as he rode away, he looked over his shoulder.

They watched him, then loped back toward the house, stopping once or twice to sniff something dropped, something new.

Then they were gone.

24

ON MONDAY, when he delivered the papers, he threw old man Cruz's paper down the dark bend in the road, because even though he knew that the Cruz dogs were okay, there were still the jungle dogs.

When he was done, Boy stopped at the viewpoint and sat on his bike. All save a few stars had faded away, and along the beach a handful of house lights reflected tiny pinpoints on his silver handlebars.

The glow on the far horizon grew bold and wide, and rays of gold fanned above it and spread over the sea. Boy stuck out his hand to trace the thin line between sea and sky, following it past the flat island, the far ocean, the marine base, and back down along the coast to where he stood.

Below on the sand Buzzy worked his canoe across the sand to the water. Boy dropped his bike and hurried down the slope in a landslide of dust and dirt, running past Gilbert, who was shouting, "Prepare the lifeboats!"

"Buzzy," he called.

"Hey," Buzzy said. "What you so excited about?"

Boy bent over to catch his breath. "I don't know. . . . I just . . . feel good."

"Well, hop in, then."

Boy climbed aboard the canoe and Buzzy pushed it out and jumped in himself. They paddled toward the flat island.

For a time they were silent. Ocean water whirlpooled around each thrust and pull. For now, they alone were in the world.

Once around the island, Boy said, "If somebody asked you who you looked up to, what would you say?"

"How come you ask that?"

"My teacher made us write about who we look up to in our life, like somebody we admire."

Buzzy paddled. Boy studied him from behind, the thin back, the muscles and dark, glistening skin.

"Chee," Buzzy said. "I had lots of people in my life I looked up to. Hard to answer that. Do they have to be alive?"

"I guess not."

"Okay, then. For me I think I would have to say it was the guy who thought up this boat."

"But that was you. You made it."

"No-no, I mean the guy who first thought of how to make a canoe, way back in the olden days, probably almost back to caveman days. You see, sometimes when I'm out here in this canoe, I think about that first guy, and all the guys after him who made the first canoe better, and all of them who passed down how to make canoes. Funny, but I feel like all those guys and me are connected by that one idea: the canoe. They passed this down to me. I think about how what I am—and what you are too—is made up of all those guys that came before us. They got us to where we are today, yeah? And we got to take that and make it a little better, then pass it on to the next guys. So, if you ask me who I look up to, then I would have to say it ain't just one guy. It's all those ones."

Boy considered what Buzzy had said: all the guys who came before.

"Huh," Buzzy said, breaking the silence. "Crazy what you think about out here on the water, yeah?"

"Buzzy . . ."

"What?"

"You got a family?"

Buzzy stopped paddling and looked back over his shoulder. "What?"

"Do you have brothers and sisters? A family."

Buzzy turned and started paddling again. "Sure I got a family. Everybody got a family. My mama passed on about eight years ago. My papa, two years after that. He and Mama were very close.

"And I got a brother, Mike. He lives in Utah."

"Utah?"

"He's a Mormon."

"What's a Mormon?"

"It's a religion. Nice people."

"Are you a Mormon?"

"No, no, not me." He laughed, then added, "I'm a heathen. I got my own religion—the ocean."

"Is Mike older than you?"

"Younger. I'm the old guy."

They paddled in silence, Boy scowling. "Do you like your brother?"

Buzzy stopped paddling and turned around in his seat. He put the paddle across his knees. "How come you so interested in me and my family?"

"I don't know." Boy looked toward the island.

Buzzy chuckled and said, "S' okay, Boy. I'll tell you. Me and Mike were always different. He was smart, liked school, got good grades. And me, I was always outside, in this canoe, fishing, hiking in the mountains. Mike didn't like that kind of thing. But we were still close. In our whole life we never got into one fight. I think it was because he was just a nice guy, you know. Wouldn't even hurt a cockaroach. But me, if I see a cockaroach, I would whack 'um with a newspaper.''

Buzzy laughed and rubbed his neck with his hand. "When we got older, he went one way and I went another. So why you asking all these questions?''

"Because of school. Because of that thing I gotta write. I can't think of anyone.''

"Doesn't sound so hard to me,'' Buzzy said.

"No . . . But it is.''

Buzzy looked at his feet, nodding.

Boy said, "I wrote about my dog.''

Buzzy laughed. "Your *dog*?''

"I don't even have a dog.''

Buzzy scratched his whiskery chin. "You just made it up?''

"Yeah.''

"You don't look up to anyone in your family?''

"I think I do, but . . . I don't know.''

"That doesn't make sense, Boy.''

"I know. That's why I was asking about your family, I guess.''

Buzzy bent forward, putting his elbows on his knees. "I tell you about my brother. He's the one I would say was the one I look up to. And you know why? Because he ain't afraid to be himself.

"You see, my family, when we grew up, we

were Buddhists, yeah? And then one day when he was in high school, Mike met up with those guys that ride around on the bikes, those ones wear white shirts and a tie. Mormons.

"Well, Mike and those guys made friends. Spent a lot of time together. Papa used to *scowl* when he saw them coming. They used to try to talk to me, too, but I didn't have the time. I rather go fishing, or go in my canoe, or something like that.

"Anyways, they kept coming back, coming back, talking to Mike. Sometimes Mike went places with them at night. And then he started going to church with them on Sundays. And . . ."

Buzzy opened his hands, like saying, It was bound to happen. ". . . And pretty soon Mike came home and told Papa he was going be baptized, become a Mormon.

"*Ho*, did my old man get *mad*! Mama was upset, too, but of course she didn't say anything, not while Papa was talking. Papa told Mike, 'If you get baptized, then *leave* this house. Go find somewheres else to live. How can you shun your family like this? How can you shun where you come from?' "

Boy thought of Daddy yelling at Damon. He could almost hear his fist hit the table, the silverware bouncing.

Buzzy shook his head. "And you know what Mike said? And remember, this kid was only about tenth grade at the time. He looked my old man straight in the eye and he said: 'Papa, I love this family. You and Mama mean everything to me. But I found something else, too. Something that makes me feel good inside, something that makes me happy. I have to do it, Papa. I was hoping you would be there.'

"The *silence* after that . . . Papa wouldn't even *look* at him. *Mama* wouldn't look at him.

"I got up to sneak away, but Mike said, 'Buzzy, you'll be there, won't you?'

"Shee. I was caught, yeah? In the middle. I looked at Papa, who glared slit eyes at me. Mama wouldn't look at anyone. I looked at Mike. Then Papa. Then Mike again.

"Finally, I said, 'Sorry, Mike.' That's what I said, ''Sorry, Mike.' "

Buzzy studied his rough hands.

"All Mike did was nod. He never bothered me about that again, never treated me any different. He just accepted that I wasn't going to be there.

"Of course Papa was happy about that, and I was happy that Papa wasn't mad at me, too.

"So you see, Mike had the guts. Me? I was a coward. Inside, I wanted to go see him get baptized, because that's what he wanted."

Buzzy bowed his head and ran his hand

through his short white hair. "And I didn't have the guts to go. All my life I've felt bad about that. All my life. And till the day he died, Papa never understood. But Mike always treated him the same."

Buzzy sat up. "My brother has class, Boy. Class."

Boy and Buzzy sat a moment, staring at the half inch of seawater sloshing around their feet.

Finally, Buzzy took his paddle and turned around. "Let's go," he said, "before we dry out."

They paddled.

Boy thought about Mike. He wished he could say Damon had class, too, like Mike. But Damon wasn't that kind of guy. But he could be, Boy thought. If he wanted to. If he told those Cuda guys to take a hike.

Buzzy stopped paddling and looked back. "You couldn't think of *one* person you look up to?"

"No."

"Even your parents?"

"I didn't think of them."

"Why not?"

"Well . . ."

"You like your parents?"

"Sure I like them."

"Without them you wouldn't be here, yeah?"

"Yeah . . ."

"So how's about them?"

Buzzy raised his eyebrows and turned back and started paddling again. They went down the coast about halfway to the marine base, then turned around and headed back. The ocean was smooth, blue-green above the sandy bottom. And with the sun in the east behind them, the island bloomed with new color—white sand, yellow-green palm trees, blue-green mountains. Big, rising sky.

But Boy saw none of it, his head crammed with thoughts.

25

ALL THE GOOD FEELINGS Boy had felt that morning did not follow him into the classroom.

First, while he was walking to school, he'd started thinking about Crowboy's tires. Crowboy would take his revenge, and just thinking that made Boy's hands shake.

Second, a spitwad hit the back of his neck the minute he sat down.

"Gabriel!" Ms. Ching said. "I saw that. You come up here. Now! And bring your essay with you."

He glared at Ms. Ching, then slammed his hand on his desk and pushed himself up. He ripped a piece of paper out of his notebook and walked toward the front of the room, bumping Boy's desk as he went by.

He thinks he's so cool, Boy thought.

Gabriel slouched up to Ms. Ching and stood in

front of the class with a look of complete irritation.

"Gabriel, would you please tell us why you are standing up here this morning."

Boy crossed his arms. Yeah, Bozo, tell us.

Gabriel mumbled, "Because I threw a piece of paper."

Ms. Ching said, "A spitwad, you mean," and the class laughed. Gabriel looked like he wanted to murder someone. "Have we talked about throwing things in class before?"

"Yeah."

"Is it something we do in this class?"

"No."

"That's right. And why?"

Gabriel shrugged. "I forget."

"Let me refresh your memory, then. It *disturbs* the class. It doesn't show *respect* for your fellow students and what they are trying to do here, which is learn something. Do you remember now?"

Gabriel nodded.

"Good. Why don't you read us your essay."

"No."

Gabriel picked off a long loose strip of spiral edging from his paper and stared at it a moment and the whole class was silent.

"Excuse me?" Ms. Ching said.

"It's a joke."

Ms. Ching paused. Would she send him to the principal? She'd never sent anyone there before.

"What's a joke?" Ms. Ching finally said.

"This stupid essay."

"You mean the assignment is a joke?"

Gabriel scowled. "No. What I wrote is a joke."

"Well, let's hear it anyway. Just for fun, if it's a joke."

Boy leaned forward and watched Gabriel squirm.

He started reading. "*I don't* . . .

"*I don't look up to anyone, except maybe Steven Seagal, who was awesome in* Out for Justice."

He looked up to glare at anyone who might laugh.

"*And I like my sister because of how she's nice to me. Her name is Anna and she's in eleventh grade at Kailua High School. When I have a problem, I can talk to her and she won't get bored. Sometimes I talk with my brother but he gets mad if I bother him. Besides, he hardly lives at our house. I don't have a father and my mother is always working. But my sister will listen when I need to tell somebody something. She is very quiet. She is . . . she is . . .*

"*She is my best friend.*"

Gabriel kept his eyes on his paper. He looked different, somehow. Boy wondered if he should feel sorry for Gabriel. That would be hard.

"That was beautiful, Gabriel," Ms. Ching said

softly. She gave him a hug, which looked funny because he was a head taller than she was.

Gabriel went back to his seat staring at the floor. He didn't bump Boy's desk.

Boy's head started to ache from thinking.

26

AFTER SCHOOL, when Boy was walking across the grass toward the high school, he saw Gabriel ahead of him. He was alone. No idiot Moose, or Barry. Boy slowed down to put more space between them.

Then he thought, No.

"Hey!" he called.

Gabriel stopped and looked back. Boy felt his stomach go sour. "Kissy boy," Gabriel said, then grinned, like here comes the lamb to get made into lamb chops.

Boy said, "I . . . I like what you wrote . . . about your sister."

Gabriel's grin vanished. He squinted at Boy, as if deciding whether or not Boy was making fun of him. Boy said, quick, "It wasn't a joke, was it? . . . Your essay."

Gabriel squinted harder. "Yeah, well, she liked Marianne's one better."

Boy nodded. "Maybe. They were different."

Gabriel studied Boy. "Well, anyway, it was better than your stupid dog one."

Boy started to grin, then stopped.

"I guess you know somebody cut my brother's tires," Gabriel said.

Boy didn't answer.

"I guess you know who that somebody was, too."

"I do?"

"He's messing with *Crowboy,* and Crowboy's gonna take his revenge."

"Just like Damon was taking his."

Gabriel hesitated, then said, "That's right."

It was weird talking to Gabriel. But not bad, really.

They both stood looking at their feet.

Gabriel sucked his teeth. Finally, he looked up. "Back and forth, back and forth, until somebody gets hurt."

Boy winced, remembering the meat rolling out of the cut on Damon's stomach, the blood he couldn't get off his hands. Back and forth until somebody *dies,* he thought.

"Somebody's got to stop it," Boy said, looking in Gabriel's eyes.

"Too late. It's already going. Anyways, you don't know Crowboy."

"Oh, I think I know Crowboy."

"Yeah. You prob'ly do."

"Well . . . somebody has to stop them."

"Why?"

Boy pursed his lips, looked down, then back up. "What if it's *your* brother who gets hurt next time? What if Damon . . ." He stopped and shook his head.

Gabriel glanced toward the high school and the cars pulling out of the parking lot. Still looking that way, he said, "You know, Henry ain't so bad."

"*Henry*. That's his name?"

"He hates it."

"I don't like mine, either."

Gabriel grinned. "Yeah, it is kind of stupid."

"My brother," Boy said, then paused. "You . . . you know, he's not so bad, either. Actually, he's a pretty nice guy."

"So nice he cut somebody's tires."

"That was stupid."

"You right there, brah."

"But your brother cut *him*."

Gabriel blinked, and said, "He said it was an accident. He only wanted to scare him."

"With a knife?"

"Hey, your brother crossed him, man, and Henry don't sit around for that. He ain't that kind of person, he don't take that."

"See. Back and forth."

Gabriel looked away.

"It's because of us, you know," Boy said. "You and me."

"So?" Gabriel turned back.

"So that doesn't bother you?"

"Why should it? That's their problem, not mine."

"Well . . . what if somebody *really* got hurt, like died, even?"

Gabriel spit. "Too late. Nobody can stop them. Not now."

"Why not?"

"Are you *stupid*? Your brother cut up his *tires*, man. Act of war. You think Crowboy going let that go because somebody says to stop? *Shhh*. You dreaming, bug eyes. Anyways, I don't like you."

Above in the blue a small bird flew by with a silver gum wrapper in its beak. Boy and Gabriel watched it until it landed on the roof of the high school.

"Shee," Gabriel said. "What he going do with one gum wrapper?"

They moved on, heading home, for the first time in their lives walking together.

"What did I ever do to you?" Boy said.

Gabriel didn't answer for a while. Finally, he said, "I don't know."

When they'd gone past the high school to the intersection where they would go in different directions, they stopped. Boy said, "I don't like you, either . . . but that doesn't mean it has to stay that way."

Gabriel turned to spit.

Just like Damon, Boy thought. Always spitting. Boy said, "Maybe we can make a truce, you and me. Tell our brothers to stay out of it."

"Why?"

"Why not?"

Gabriel looked at Boy, eyes cool. "I'll think about it."

Boy held out a fist.

Gabriel looked at it a long moment. He nodded and gently tapped Boy's fist with his own. "This don't mean nothing," he said. "I'm just thinking about it."

"Fine," Boy said.

27

AT 4:55 THE FOLLOWING MORNING Boy sat on his bike with one foot on the ground, staring down the road to the Cruz place. He was feeling pretty good because last night he'd written a new essay, and then he'd rewritten it until it felt right.

He heard a whisper of wind and ducked. A bat *whoomp*ed past and vanished behind him.

Boy listened to the bushes.

But the bushes were silent. And the road before him lay deep and dark.

He pushed the bike forward, then stood on the pedals and coasted down with only the crunching sound of dirt and rock popping under his tires. He crept around the bend into the dead spot where neither the street nor the house could be seen.

He stopped.

He sat with one foot on the ground and the other on the pedal, ready to run.

Sandpapery bumps rose on his arms.

A whisper of padded feet.

A rustle of brush.

His hands started to tremble, and he gripped the handlebar tighter. But the shaking was not something he had charge over. The order was sent from some faraway place within him, from the memory of the chain-link fence. Boy could see the leaping dog, the snapping teeth, the yellow-red eyes.

He listened, but now could hear nothing beyond the beat of his pulse in his ears. He squinted into the blackness, leaning over the handlebars to see, and a dark shape came out onto the road.

A dog.

Not a Cruz dog—it wasn't big enough. There was enough light now for Boy to see the lay of the head, the stance, the ratty brown fur and the sticklike legs.

The dog studied Boy, then dipped its head and paced to the left, then paced back and stopped and looked at Boy. Behind it another dog came out. Then another and another and another until there were six.

Boy couldn't say, Good dog. He couldn't even click his tongue or put his bike between them as a shield.

One dog growled.

At that moment one of the Cruz dogs barked.

The six dogs flinched like the sudden sound was a gunshot. The growling stopped.

". . . It's okay," Boy squeaked. "Nobody's going to hurt you."

At the sound of his voice, the dogs vanished, weaving into the fabric of shadows and trees. Gone, *poof,* like they had never been there.

Boy gulped. *Jungle dogs.* The dread gushed out of him in waves of relief until his rubbery legs nearly betrayed him.

He stood there and remembered the pit bull slamming into the fence. But this time another part of that memory came with it, one he had never remembered before. There was a girl. A small dirty-faced girl, maybe four or five years old. She was . . . she was in the rusty car with no wheels . . . playing . . . in the yard. And the dog did not snarl at her, or charge her. The dog did not want to kill her.

But he knew it wanted to kill *him.*

Boy turned his bike toward the Cruz house. Maybe, he thought, this was like what Buzzy had said, about how people are afraid of things they don't understand.

Was this like that? The girl knew the dog and he didn't, so he was afraid and she wasn't?

Maybe.

He pushed off and rode toward the Cruz house. The old man's dogs came running out.

They barked before recognizing him, then gathered around his legs with wagging tails and wet noses and followed him up to the house.

Boy dropped a paper on the bottom step.

Then he turned and rode back out to the street.

Boy finished delivering his papers and raced home. He didn't stop and look out at the ocean, at the beauty that would be there no matter what good or bad thing was going on at any time anywhere in the world. There was no time.

He had to tell Damon *now*. It didn't *have* to be fight or die. Damon and Crowboy didn't *have* to fight like Gabriel had said. Always Boy had known it didn't have to be like that, but he'd never known why, only what Damon had told him—you coward, you sissy, you pantieboy, you got to get some guts, they going eat you eat you *eat* you— and he could never explain how he felt, even to himself.

But now he thought: If Damon could get to know Crowboy like the little girl knew the dog, and if they could talk and work it out like he and Gabriel were trying to do, then no one would have to fight, no one would have to get hurt, or die, and they could end it.

Before it was too late.

28

BUT WHEN HE GOT HOME, Damon had already left for school. And after school, Boy couldn't find him.

And Damon didn't come home for dinner, which made Daddy frown and worried Mama, and Venita was annoyed by how everyone was making such a big thing out of nothing.

Long after everyone had gone to sleep, Venita opened the door to Boy's room and turned on the light.

Boy popped up and squinted.

"The phone's for you," Venita said. "Tell your friend not to call so late. It's after midnight!"

"What?" Boy said, trying to wake up.

"The phone. Get it in the kitchen." She turned the light off and left.

Boy stumbled out and picked up the phone. "Hello?" he said.

"They going meet on the beach . . . at one o'clock."

"Gabriel?"

"One o'clock, tonight. Crowboy and Damon going fight. At the beach. Lot of guys going be there."

Gabriel hung up.

Mama came out. "Was that Damon?"

"Uh . . . no. Just somebody looking for him."

Mama shook her head and went back to her room. Poor Mama. Boy couldn't hear Daddy snoring and wondered if he was awake, too. He thought about telling him about the phone call. No. No, no. Maybe he should, but Daddy might make it worse.

Boy dressed quickly.

At 12:15 he slipped out the kitchen door, a quiet door that didn't squeak like the front one. A bright white quarter moon spread eerie shadows across the yard.

Boy crept toward the street, passing on the far side of Daddy's truck in case Mama was looking out the window. He thought he heard the phone again. He stopped and listened. A car came down the road toward him. Boy jumped behind a tree and stood as still as a lizard until it passed.

When the car was gone, he ran across the street to the beach park. He ran through the parking lot and up the grassy hill and over to the long moonlit beach.

No one.

But it wasn't one o'clock yet.

Would Gabriel show up? Or had he lied, just to make him worry? But Gabriel wouldn't do that, not after they'd talked. He had to believe Gabriel wasn't as bad as that.

He walked down to the easy surf *foomp*ing on the sand. Warm, soothing water rushed up and over his feet. The light from a small boat winked far at sea, on, off, on, off. Maybe the ocean was rough out there.

He decided to walk down the beach toward the marine base. It was so strange to think of hating and fighting, and at the same time have all around him the peaceful island, the silvery sea and quiet, starry universe.

Only a handful of house lights glowed down along the coast. Must be about 12:30 by now.

He headed into the ironwood trees and hid in the shadows.

If Damon was going to fight, Boy would stop him. A crazy idea, but it was *his* fault that Damon was there, or at least it was partly. The rest of it was Damon's dumb fight or die thing. Where he got that—who could say? Small kids didn't fight or die. Daddy and his friends didn't fight or die. How come it was only like that with the young guys? And how come it was only *guys* who believed in that? How come girls didn't?

He saw Crowboy's gang first.

He could tell it was them because there were ten of them. And Damon didn't have ten friends, let alone ten Cudas.

They were way down the beach. Was Gabriel one of them? No. Crowboy wouldn't allow that. Too much stupid pride to let his little brother in on something like this.

The shadowy mass grew larger as they came closer, dark silhouetted bobbing heads.

No sound but the ocean. On and on and on.

Fooomp. Shhhhhh.

Fooomp. Shhhhhh.

Moving dark shapes. Coming closer.

Boy inched back into the shadows of the trees. He held his breath, afraid to even blink.

Soon he heard their voices, mumbling low.

He turned and looked toward the pavilion.

No Damon.

He looked back at Crowboy's guys, coming closer.

Then back to the pavilion and this time he saw Damon and the Cudas—one, two, three, four. That was all.

Damon was walking into a slaughter! Boy tried

to think. Should I duck out and tell him to run for it? Should I stay here and see what happens? Maybe Crowboy will take pity on the Cudas, the little-boy Cudas, the four measly little-boy Cudas.

Crowboy's gang stopped, now quiet.

The Cudas walked up the hill of grass and stopped at the top and looked down on the silvery gray beach. Four black figures outlined against the moon-bright sky.

Freeze, Damon. Maybe they won't see you.

But one of Crowboy's guys spotted them. They spread out along the beach and faced the Cudas.

Boy hunched over and duck-walked to another tree, closer.

Crowboy called to Damon, "What you punks waiting for? You going run?"

Slowly, the Cudas headed down to the sand, walking toward the ten guys. Halfway there, Bobby and Joker stopped. Only Rick and Damon went all the way down to them.

Crowboy swung. *Fop!* Damon hit the sand.

Bobby and Joker ran back up into the trees and kept going.

Two of Crowboy's guys tried to grab Rick, but he broke free and ran, too.

Damon scrambled up. He raised a piece of pipe.

Boy stood. Step in. Do it. *"Stop!"* he yelled.

Damon turned, and when he saw it was Boy,

he shouted, "Get out of here!" and raised the pipe as if to hit his own brother. Boy kept coming.

"What is this?" Crowboy said. "Who invited you?"

"Leave Damon alone!" Boy said. "Me and Gabriel can take care of ourselves."

"This is way past you guys now. So beat it. Before I get mad."

"No," Boy said.

Crowboy laughed. "What?"

Damon shoved Boy aside and raised the pipe. "Come on," he said to Crowboy.

"You need that thing to fight? You need a weapon?"

Damon swung the pipe.

Crowboy jumped away and grinned. "Missed."

Somebody said, "If you see fog approaching, fix your position, or take a bearing. If possible, find . . ."

Crowboy looked up. "What the—?"

Everyone turned around. Someone was walking toward them.

". . . Remember to ring your bell for about five seconds every minute, and keep a sharp listening watch. If at anchor . . ."

"Who's that?" Crowboy said.

Gilbert stopped and looked up, startled. He hadn't even seen them. He started to back away.

"Get outta here, bum," Crowboy said.

Gilbert turned and hurried off.

"I can't believe it," Crowboy said. "First the midget, then the idiot. Who's *next*? Don't nobody sleep around here?"

Damon waited, the pipe ready.

Boy stepped between them.

Crowboy hit his shoulder and knocked him down. "I *had* it with you."

Damon came at Crowboy, swinging.

Crowboy grabbed his arm, ripped the pipe away, and flipped it into the ocean.

Damon's fist lashed out and grazed Crowboy's cheek.

Boy struggled up and worked his way between them, Damon still swinging. Boy took one of his blows and stumbled back.

Crowboy knocked Damon down and three guys swarmed all over him.

Boy jumped in again.

"You one stupid little fut, you know?" *Whop!* Crowboy sent him flying with a slap to his face.

Boy fell and grabbed his cheek. Little white stars popped in his brain. Tears gathered in his eyes. He got up and came back.

Crowboy pushed him down and kicked his legs.

Boy cried out. He crawled back. He got to his knees, and stood.

"Are you *mental*?" Crowboy yelled in Boy's face, then thumped his chest with both hands, hard, and again Boy fell to the sand.

Boy got up.

Crowboy kneed him in the stomach.

Boy fell and got up on his hands and knees.

"Leave him alone," Damon said. "I'll *kill* you."

Boy crawled to Crowboy.

Crowboy knelt down, and said, "Listen, just get out of here, man. What are you trying to do?"

Boy shook his head.

Crowboy shoved him aside and walked over to Damon. "Your brother's got more guts than you, you know that? Ten times more. You sneak around at night and cut up people's cars. You ain't no man. He's a man."

Damon glared at Crowboy.

Whap! Crowboy slapped Damon's head by his ear. "That's for my tires." He looked back at Boy and raised his hand.

Boy didn't duck. Too dizzy.

"Tst," Crowboy spit.

A man came out of the shadows.

Daddy.

When he saw Boy all woozy on his knees, he started for Crowboy, but Crowboy's guys stepped up and blocked him.

Daddy stood for a moment, glaring, breathing

hard. Finally, he said, "These are my sons and I'm taking them home."

Crowboy laughed. "You wrong, old man. Me and Damon's got business."

Daddy said, "You really want the police on your back again? Because if you don't let my boys go, you're going to have a mountain of them coming down on you."

"Shuddup!" Crowboy spit. "I ain't afraid of cops or you. Now get out of here or else we going take you, too."

Daddy said, "Your mama must be real proud of you, huh? Going out at night with all these tough guys to find younger boys to push around."

"I said *shuddup*! Get him out of here," Crowboy said, and two guys grabbed Daddy.

Big mistake.

Bim! Bam! Both of them went down, Daddy twisting their arms while they yelled, *"Ahhhh!"* for him to let go.

Damon looked like he couldn't believe what he just saw. Boy's eyes popped, too.

Crowboy charged Daddy, and Daddy let go of the other guys and stepped aside as Crowboy came at him. Crowboy tripped and scrambled back up.

"One last time," Daddy said. "You boys go home and I won't tell no cops about this. And don't you worry. I know who you are. I know

some of you are on probation. *You*—Johnny
Thompson's boy. *You*—your father is Stan Choi,
works at the Bank of Hawaii. You and you and
you, I know *all* your fathers."

One, two of Crowboy's guys started to back
away, mumbling to Crowboy. Then one more,
and now there were only Crowboy and six guys.

Crowboy said to Daddy, "He cut up my tires
and he going pay. If not tonight, then some other
time."

"He did *what?*" Daddy said.

"Cut up my tires, all four of them."

There was a silence.

Fooomp. Shhhhhh.

"How much?" Daddy said. "What they cost?"

"Hundred bucks each."

Daddy looked at Damon and said, "Then he'll
pay you four hundred." He turned back to
Crowboy. "If you get that, you stop this fighting?"

Crowboy paused, then said, "Yeah, fine. Four
hundred. Cash. Tomorrow. I get that, I leave him
alone."

"You'll get it," Daddy said.

"I better get it, old man."

Daddy put one hand on Damon's shoulder
and the other on Boy's and waited for Crowboy's
guys to step aside.

The three of them walked up the sand to the
trees, and when they were over the hill, Boy fell to

his knees, bent over, and threw up. He coughed and spit and threw up some more.

Daddy knelt beside him and put a hand on his back. Damon scowled toward the beach.

Boy looked up and saw a boy in the tree shadows. The boy stepped back, then ran off. Gabriel.

"Son?" Daddy said.

"Huh?"

"You ready?"

"How . . . how did you know we were here?"

"I didn't. I went looking for you. Venita saw that you weren't in your bed, and woke me. You should have come to me, Boy."

Boy coughed, and tasted the sourness on his tongue.

Daddy started to help him up, but Damon touched Daddy's arm. "I'll do it."

Damon bent over and put his hand on Boy's elbow.

Boy looked up.

"Let's go home, bro."

29

Boy SLEPT TWO HOURS, then got up to deliver papers.

He sat on the edge of his bed with his eyes still closed. He felt a mild pain in his stomach and in his legs where he'd been kicked. And his face hurt where Crowboy had slapped him. But it wasn't that bad. He'd been pretty lucky, he figured.

He opened his eyes, and when he did, he saw Damon sitting over on his bed, looking at him. Damon had taken the bandage off his stomach. Now there was only a dark scabby scar with the stitches still in it.

Boy got dressed and went out to get the papers.

Minutes later Damon came and sat down next to him and they folded the papers in silence. They put them in Boy's bike bag and Boy delivered them, even old man Cruz's paper, which he took all the way to the doorstep while Damon waited.

Then Boy and Damon rode in silence to the viewpoint, where they stopped and looked out.

"I got a hundred seventy-eight dollars saved up," Boy said. "You can have it."

Damon sat on his bike with his feet on the ground, not looking at Boy.

"You can pay me back later."

"I don't need your money. After you went to sleep last night, the old ma—Daddy and I had a talk. He said he'd pay it."

Boy studied Damon. Where could Daddy ever get four hundred dollars by the end of the day? Where could all of them put *together* get it?

"I told him don't pity me. I'd get the money."

"Damon, why you always say things like that to make him mad?"

"He said it wasn't pity. It was . . . it was something I'd understand when I had a son of my own. If I lived that long."

Damon turned his bike to leave. "Tomorrow you on your own, little man."

Boy watched his brother coast down the road. *Brother.*

That word felt good again. Like *Mama* or *Daddy,* or *sister.*

30

BOY WAS LATE FOR CLASS.

He carried his math book with his new essay folded inside it.

Gabriel watched him walk in, but shifted his eyes when Boy caught him looking.

Ms. Ching stopped in the middle of a sentence and waited. Boy walked to his desk, slower than usual. He still trembled from the night before, short shudders that swept over him for no reason at all.

After he sat down, Ms. Ching said, "Everyone, please take out your essays."

Groans rippled through the room. Nobody was in much of a hurry. Boy looked at his hands as if by doing so he could stop the quivering and the dull ache in his stomach and head.

But deep inside, where it mattered, he was calm. Like he didn't have to hurry or worry or anything. Just sit there feeling peaceful.

Trembling on the outside and calm inside. Weird.

"I'm going to give you fifteen minutes to look them over," Ms. Ching went on. "Make any changes or corrections you wish. Then I'm going to collect them and read them and when you come back after lunch I might read one or two of them to the class."

Folders popped open.

Boy took his essay out of the math book—his new essay that he'd written and rewritten all the way up until that morning. On the top he tried to draw a cube, but it came out wobbly. He erased it as Ms. Ching collected the essays.

It was pizza day in the cafeteria. Boy and Zeke sat with their brown plastic trays at a corner table and shoveled the pizza down in less than a minute. They wiped their oily fingers on their shirts, then drank their milk in silence. It was hot out, really hot. Flies. Volcano sun.

"What's the matter?" Zeke said. "You're kind of quiet today."

"I'm just tired."

"The paper job?"

"Yeah, the paper job."

Zeke took a swig of milk and made a gagging face. "*Ahhchh.* I *hate* milk."

"I like it."

"You *like* it. You're crazy."

But they both liked the chocolate chip cookie.

Four tables down, Gabriel and his friends broke out laughing and Zeke and Boy looked up.

"Don't let him get to you," Zeke said.

"He doesn't."

"Like somebody's gum, yeah? Stuck to your foot."

Boy grinned. "Sometimes, yeah."

After lunch and a recess break, they all sat hot and sweaty at their desks.

Boy started to draw a knife, but stopped and put the paper back in his desk. He didn't feel like drawing anything.

Ms. Ching faced the class. "Overall, your essays were very, very good."

Relief whispered around the room.

"I'd like to read one to you," Ms. Ching said. "This student did a lot of thinking for this assignment—and a lot of feeling—which is just what I was looking for. It's by Boy Regis."

Boy snapped up.

Moose squeaked, *"Arf, arf."* Some of the people around him muffled laughs but shut up when Ms. Ching glared at them. Boy noticed that Gabriel hadn't been one of them.

Ms. Ching started reading.

"I look up to nobody. And everybody."

"Hey, what happened to the dog?" Gabriel said, and everyone laughed.

"Often our first ideas are not our best ideas, Gabriel. May I continue?"

Gabriel sank into his chair, almost sliding under his desk.

Boy stared at his hands. He still couldn't believe what Daddy had done. And what *he* had done. And what *Damon* had done. Being nice. This morning he'd even put on a blue T-shirt. *Blue!*

Ms. Ching continued reading Boy's essay.

"I look up to nobody. And everybody.

"Nobody, because nobody's perfect. And everybody, because I think everyone has something worth looking up to inside them.

"I look up to my father, who works hard for his family and fights with his kids because he loves them and wants them to have a good life.

"I look up to a friend who stood up for me and got beat up because of it.

"I look up to an old man who is afraid of dying, but is learning to understand it so that when the time comes, he will not be afraid.

"I look up to my mother, whose life is hard because she has five kids, yet for each of us she finds what is good and thinks about that.

181

"I look up to my sister, who cared enough to choose a good boyfriend, a boy some people think is strange, but who really isn't, and she could tell.

"I even look up to a boy I don't like very much, because inside I know he cares about things."

Boy peeked over at Gabriel, who sat staring at his desk.

"I also look up to a man who keeps his mother happy by chasing midgets out of her yard."

This made the class roar with laughter, even Ms. Ching. "We'll ask Boy about that one later," she said.

"I look up to my teacher, who cares about kids.

"And I look up to my older brother, because even though he can drive me crazy, he has always watched out for me. And someday I'm going to tell him I look up to him, because fifty years from now I don't want it to be something I wish I'd said but didn't.

"So I guess, to me, what makes a person worth looking up to isn't so much the good things that they do, but that they do something good at all."

Ms. Ching looked up, then walked over to Boy's desk and put her hand on top of his head. She started to speak, but changed her mind and went back to the front of the room and said, "Please take out your math books."

While everyone mumbled and screeched their chairs and thumped their books on the desks, a spitwad hit Boy's ear.

He looked back.

Gabriel flicked his eyebrows.

Boy shook his head. Then he made a fist and ground it into his hand.

And Gabriel grinned. He tried not to, but there it was.

About the Author

Graham Salisbury is a descendant of the Thurston and Andrews families, some of the first missionaries to arrive in the Hawaiian Islands. He grew up on Oahu and on Hawaii. He graduated from California State University and received an M.F.A. from Vermont College of Norwich University. He lives with his family in Portland, Oregon, where he manages a historic office building.

His first novel, *Blue Skin of the Sea,* won the Bank Street Child Study Association Children's Book Award, the PEN/Norma Klein Award, the Judy Lopez Award, and the Oregon Book Award and was selected as an ALA Best Book for Young Adults. *Under the Blood-Red Sun* won the Scott O'Dell Award for Historical Fiction and the Oregon Book Award and was an ALA Notable Book and Best Book for Young Adults. Graham Salisbury's most recent novel, *Shark Bait,* was selected as a *Parents' Choice* Silver Honor Book.